SPEAR CREEK

STEVEN J TAYLOR

SEVERED PRESS

HOBART TASMANIA

SPEAR CREEK

Copyright © 2020 Steven J Taylor
Copyright © 2020 by Severed Press

WWW.SEVEREDPRESS.COM

ISBN: 978-1-922551-46-7

For my wife, Carolina, with whom I hope to one day retire and travel to every corner of Australia with.

1

"Pull over now. I've got a bar."

I checked the mirrors and eased the motorhome onto the shoulder of the road before gently pulling to a stop. The mirror check was not necessary. There were no cars on the roads today. We had not seen a single vehicle since the morning.

I turned and stared anxiously at my wife. "Do you still have that bar?"

She nodded. Her eyes were fixed on the phone intently. She was concentrating hard, as though dropping her guard for a moment would see the faint glimmer of a network signal disappear.

"You know," I said, my voice now playfully seductive, "we are alone in the wilderness. We have a bed in the back, and I can see down your shirt. You're looking very attractive right now, Hot Lips. I am starting to get a bar of my own."

I placed my hand gently on her thigh and slowly slid my hand up.

She half smiled and slapped my hand away. "Stop it. It's late in the day and we have to find somewhere to stop for the night. I don't want to be sleeping parked on the side of the road in the middle of nowhere without power or water."

I clutched my heart and let out an exaggerated sigh. She was right, of course. It was too late for friskiness now and we could not turn back for Adelaide either. It would be late at night when we arrived, and there was no guarantee that there were any sites available for us when we got there. Many places had already begun turning customers away. No one new in.

Earlier today, the Australian government had called for a total lockdown to stop the spread of the pandemic. It was not unexpected it would come to this. Internationally we had already seen other countries go into lockdown to get the virus under control. Pre-lockdown panic buying had already hit top gear across supermarkets nationally, particularly for toilet paper (of all things!). I had never seen anything like it. Whole toilet paper shelves were empty in all the stores. The news even showed footage of people fighting in stores over toilet paper rolls. Madness. Would a clean butt somehow prevent the virus? Or was it the virus threat causing people to crap themselves? I could only wonder.

We had been warned the lockdown was coming, but we took the risk regardless. Our daughter, Jane, was pregnant and due to give birth in a month. We were driving across Australia, aiming to arrive at Jane's house two weeks before the due date. We needed to keep moving. We were still half a country away and there was no way we were going to miss the birth of our first grandchild. Especially not Margaret. It was all she talked about. We had a suitcase full of baby clothes she had accumulated from every children's clothing shop from every town we had visited since leaving Melbourne. The collection was almost at the point of ridiculousness, the baby would probably outgrow most before they were ever worn. But I was not going to stop Margaret from shopping when it made her so happy. Even if it meant the child had more clothes than me.

A whine from beside me let me know Maisy was becoming impatient with the wait. I scratched behind her ear and she thumped her tail against the seat in appreciation.

"Anything yet?" I asked.

"No, it's very slow."

"I might let Maisy out for a run then."

"Good idea."

I checked the mirror but the roads were empty stretching to each horizon. I eased myself down from the motorhome and called Maisy. She jumped down with enthusiasm.

The area I had pulled over in was much the same as the rest of the faceless landscape we had been seeing since leaving civilisation. Tall dry grass, browned by the burning summer sun, stood tall in plains stretching out all the way to the coast on our left. The plains were broken only by trees, which clustered oddly together in clumps like cliques at an office party. On our right, a low mountain range stretched out like a poolside sunbather, also tanned brown. Everything looked so damn dry. It was no wonder bushfires spread so quickly across these open lands.

Maisy sniffed at some animal excrement on the side of the road before squatting to urinate on it. She looked up at me, appearing as though I should give her praise on a job well done. Dogs were such strange creatures at times. Satisfied with how she had left her mark, she then disappeared into the grass, only to be seen a moment later leaping above the grasses to chomp at a flying insect.

Maisy, of course, was part of the problem we had. We had passed parks with vacancies on the way, but none of them welcomed pets. We needed a campground or caravan park that welcomed pets, and right now those were at a premium.

As I watched Maisy frolic through the grass, I heard the window of the motorhome open behind me.

"The network is too slow," Margaret called to me. "I'm going to call Jane, maybe she can look it up quicker for us. Do you want to come in?"

I heaved a sigh. "I really want to, you know that, but it's she who won't speak to me. Remember last time, she wouldn't even talk to you until I had left. Don't give her cause to be upset with you too."

Margaret frowned. I knew she was struggling with it almost as much as I was. It would be hard to be stuck in the middle of a conflict between the two people you love the most. I always tiptoed around the subject, tried not to let on how deeply it hurt, lest it become a burden to Margaret as well. And I can tell you, it hurt a damn lot, but this was my cross to bear, not Margaret's.

"Don't you at least want to hear her voice? I won't let on that you are here."

"No, best not," I said, turning away to hide the tears that had begun to well in my eyes.

Jane had not spoken to me for four months now. All for one silly remark. Well, it was not silly to her. It was meant as a joke. It should have been nothing. But my daughter, and her partner Zheng, were deeply hurt by the remark and had not spoken to me since those fateful words. My apologies fell on deaf ears, and Jane would not even talk to Margaret on the phone without first confirming I was not there.

It often kept me up at night wondering what would happen when we finally did arrive in Perth. Would she see me? Would she let me see or hold the baby? It would be hard on me if she refused, but I would accept it. At least that's what I keep telling myself.

Jane had lived in Perth, the opposite end of the country, for five years now. Margaret and I had remained in our family home after Jane moved out, despite it being too big for just the two of us. We were getting older now, and the cleaning was becoming too much of a strain for both of us. We had been talking, for some time, about retiring early, buying a motorhome and travelling across Australia. We had never explored much of Australia in our lives, visiting just the typical tourist traps of the Gold Coast and Sydney, and little else. There was so much we had not seen in our own backyard and we needed to see it before it was too late.

I most definitely had had enough of working, and an early retirement made sense for me. I did not want to be too old to properly enjoy this trip. Plus, Margaret's knee was starting to become a problem. It was an old injury from her netball playing days, and she was slowly becoming less mobile because of it. We were fifty-seven years old and had spent most of our lives living in Melbourne. The time had come. We needed to bite the bullet and do it now or cross that dream off our list.

So, we did it. We made the decision to become what was now termed as 'grey nomads'. We sold the family home and purchased our new mobile home. Our life's collection of belongings, that which we could not bring, were packed into a shipping container and stored in a warehouse back in Melbourne while we explored Australia for the next year or more. It had always been a dream to drive around Australia in a motorhome, and it felt good when we finally committed to it.

When Jane announced her pregnancy, we were delighted and accelerated our plans. We were not going to miss the birth. We replanned our trip, heading west from Melbourne first with the aim to arrive in Perth two weeks before the due date. After staying in Perth a while, we would then break away and explore the rest of

Australia at leisure. A plan that was now thrown in jeopardy by a pandemic and lockdown.

But the pandemic was making getting to Perth more troublesome. We decided to leave Adelaide today and get as close to Perth as we could before lockdowns kicked in. We did not know how long a lockdown would last, but being closer would mean less distance to cover once things did reopen. But our decision seemed to have only made our situation worse, and now we were stuck in the middle of nowhere with no place to camp.

Maisy came back to me, panting and wagging her tail, obviously pleased with her work and seeking my approval. I wondered what she had done this time. A big poo perhaps? I gave her a pat and assured her that she was a good girl. It seemed to do the trick, and her ears pricked up and she dashed once more into the long grasses.

I looked up and down the empty road. Aside from the heavy traffic around the supermarkets, we had barely seen any traffic all day. It all felt very odd, and nothing like I had seen in my life before. We had seen virus scares before, but nothing that had sent cities and countries into lockdown like this. It was a little scary, but I was not sure if the virus itself was what scared me the most, or just the governments' reactions to it.

Through the open window of the motorhome cabin, I could hear Margaret talking to Jane. It sounded as though there had been some success in the web hunt, and we would have a place to stay this night. I stretched, hoping it was not a long drive ahead. I had spent most of the day seated, and I was getting a little saddle sore from the journey. Plus, I had no desire to set up the motorhome after dark.

When the call ended, I called for Maisy.

"Paul," Margaret called, "We have found a place. It's not far, but I'd like it if we could get moving straight away. Jane tried to get them on the phone but there was no answer. We need to go now and hope they have a vacancy."

I waved assent and called Maisy again and whistled. I scanned the long grass but there was no movement other than the gently swaying against the breeze. Sweat prickled my brow as I waited in the hot, dry air. I called again, but still there was no response.

"Try the dog whistle," Margaret suggested.

I felt in my pocket for it and fished it out. I gave two quick blasts. I could not hear a thing. It was one of those whistles on the frequency that people cannot hear. But Maisy heard it, and soon I could make out her form bounding through the grasses towards me. As she drew up, I could see her muzzle was covered with blood.

"What have you gotten yourself into?" I asked as I crouched to examine her. She wagged her tail and padded the ground with her front paws restlessly. I held her head and looked over her. The blood was not hers. She was not the type of dog to kill, her nature was far too kindly. She must have found something dead. But what would leave a bloodied mess behind? Perhaps there were wild dogs hereabouts. It might not have been a good idea to have let her roam freely like that.

Using a wet wipe, I cleaned her muzzle, and anywhere else where she had blood, before we got back into the motorhome.

"Right," I said as I buckled my seatbelt, "where are we going?"

"Spear Creek Farm."

"Sounds delightful," I said without a hint of the intended irony.

2

The sun was low in the sky by the time we reached Spear Creek Farm.

It was out of the way, and we had to backtrack a fair bit once we left the main road. The vegetation was thicker and plusher here, as we had moved inland and we were at the foot of the ranges which drew down the rain from the clouds. Ancient red gum trees dotted the landscape, their knotted branches curled like an old hag's hands. We saw a group of kangaroos lazing in the sun. This was quite genuinely a pretty part of Australia.

I slowed when the GPS warned us we were close, and not long after, we pulled up to the entrance of our destination. The side of the road here was topped with a barbed wire fence, and on it hung a crudely written sign pointing to a dirt road indicating where to turn for Spear Creek Farm. At the entrance was a thick, heavily reinforced stainless-steel gate, which glinted dully in the light. It was over two meters high, and came across as unnecessarily fortified. It looked at odds with the landscape, like a crude block of modernity amongst nature.

"What do you think?" I asked Margaret in a flat voice.

"I don't think anything. This was the only place Jane could fine. It will have to do."

I nodded and shrugged my shoulders. I did not like the look of the place, but as Margaret said, we did not have any other option. Any port in a storm, or so they say. I turned the motorhome onto the dirt entrance. The gate was thankfully open, and as I drove down the dirt track, passing through the gate and under the tall red gums, I felt a sudden shiver pass down my spine. I shook, but if Margaret noticed she said nothing. I ignored it and pushed on. Dirt crackled under the tires and the motorhome rocked side to side as I slowly drove down the uneven driveway.

At first glance, the so-called farm had been bereft of any semblance of farming for some time. The dirt driveway led to an old farmhouse. The house was made with brown brick with tan painted trimming and window frames. In many places the paint peeled, giving the house a general look of disrepair. The windows were grimy and curtains were drawn tight shut. The house was long and thin, and was flanked on one side by enormous water tanks, and on the other by a small open carport, and a couple of meters further on, a large shed. The carport housed a sedan that looked thirty years past its 'use by' date, and the shed was discoloured and battered. As a first impression, the farm did little to inspire.

In front of the house was the camping area, with clear spaces marked out along the ground. There was a short walk downhill to another shed which stood by a dam filled with clay brown water. All around this were empty fields of overgrown grass with not an animal in sight.

We were not going to be the only guests on the farm. In the campground ahead we could see two tents had already been set up for the night. One was quite large. Large enough to cater two people comfortably. Beside it a blue SUV was parked. The second tent was tiny. It barely stood three feet tall and seven feet long. It could only be useful for sleeping in, but I doubted it would be comfortable. I would find it constraining. Claustrophobic even. A motorcycle was parked behind it.

Three people sat on portable chairs around a small fire, all turning to watch as we approached. Beside me, Maisy had been dozing softly. A scent must have struck her, and she sniffed the air with interest, sitting up and suddenly alert, her ears cropped up.

We pulled to the front of the farmhouse in a plume of dust. As if from nowhere, a man suddenly appeared from the cloud of dust at my window, causing me to jump in fright. His face was almost a sneer, and his eyes were grey with hostility. He was unshaven, and his facial hair grew inconsistently, with some parts of his face bare and smooth and others thick with hair. His teeth were yellow and old, though the man himself seemed barely more than thirty years of age. His hair was short on the sides and long at the back, emulating the once popular mullet hairstyle. He was also rake thin, but his arms had a sinewy strength from the look of them. He was simply dressed in a grubby blue singlet and shorts.

I unwound the window, letting some of the swirling dust into the cabin. I coughed lightly, and Maisy started to softly growl. Margaret shushed her with a tap on the nose.

"Hi," I began, addressing the man, "my name is Paul Lewis." I offered my hand forward for a handshake. The man did not even bother to look down at it.

"What do yer want, Paul?" he asked in a voice as cold as the Antarctic Ocean.

I cleared my throat, my mouth suddenly dry from the dust, and I withdrew my hand.

"We wanted a place to camp for the night."

The man nodded and pointed to a space opposite the farmhouse. "Park over there then come inside for the paperwork."

As he turned away, I called out, "Ah one second, we need a lot with water and power access."

He turned back to face me, his face even less friendly than before. "Yeah, I can see that from looking at yer van. Now park *over there* like I fucking said." He raised his voice for the last part, and gestured animatedly with his finger to the spot. I turned to Margaret with one eyebrow raised. She smiled.

"He's a charmer," she said, "and quite handsome too."

"Oh, stop it" I said, shifting the motorhome back into gear.

I pulled the motorhome into a space before killing the engine. Maisy remained alert, ears cropped as she sniffed the air. I looked at Margaret doubtfully.

"Are you sure this was the only place?"

"The only one Jane could find that took pets."

"Hmmm. I can't say I like it, but it will do for one night I suppose. Hopefully we can push off tomorrow and find another spot to stay. I'll go check in with Prince Charming then come back and help set up."

As I opened the door, Maisy leapt over me and out of the cabin. I called after her, hoping she would not run. As I got down, I saw she was sniffing the ground a few feet from where we parked. Her hackles were raised as she darted back and forth. I watched her a moment, curious of her behaviour, when she stopped and stared down the farmstead towards the dam.

"What's gotten into her?" Margaret asked.

"I don't know, but can you watch her while I check in, Hot Lips?"

"Sure can, Major."

As I walked towards the farmhouse, I pulled my phone from my pocket. Zero signal. We were in another dead zone. Great.

"Hold it there, old timer," the owner called as I arrived at the open door.

I stopped, leaning forward to peer into the room through the doorway. The room was a typical entrance hall that had been roughly converted into an administration office, further evidencing that this place had once been a farm. The room had posters of Australian wildlife stuck to the walls. Some were curled at the edges, and the stains of Blu Tack were visible in the corners through the posters. Most were stuck at crude angles, as though whoever placed them took little care in the process.

The owner stood behind a counter which was untidy with paper. He was already filling a paper. He stuck his tongue out the side of his mouth as he wrote. Behind him, a key rack hung with more keys than I could imagine he would need. Above the key rack, a hunting rifle was mounted on the wall. To the man's left, a gaudy bead curtain covered the entrance to the rest of the house.

"I didn't catch your name before," I started.

"It's Bennett. Now, I need to ask you a few questions before you can come in," the owner continued. "First, have you or that woman shown any symptoms of a cold or flu in the last two weeks?"

That woman? His manner was gruff and already putting me on edge.

"That woman is my wife, and no we have not."

"No headaches, sore throats, coughs, sniffles, anything like that?"

"I've already answered you. No symptoms. We are perfectly healthy."

"Have you come into contact with anyone showing those symptoms in the last two weeks?"

"Not that I can recall. What is this all about?"

"Have you not heard there's a fucking pandemic happening? I don't need people coming in here making me sick, so are you sure you haven't come into contact with anyone with those symptoms?"

"No, we haven't."

His eyes narrowed as he regarded me cynically. It struck me then that he could quite easily reject our presence and ask us to leave, and where would we be then? We'd have to stop for the night somewhere by the side of the road, putting us in a real fix. I cleared my throat and put on a more friendly tone.

"My wife and I have kept mostly to ourselves and we are in perfect health."

He stared a moment longer, looking straight into my eyes. It took all my willpower not to look away under his hard gaze. Finally, he looked away.

"All right then, come in."

He waved me forward and I approached the counter.

"Right," he resumed, "the rules here are pretty simple. Everyone needs to be in their tents or caravans before eleven pm. No fishing or swimming in the dam. Your dog has to be tied up at night. If it shits near the other campers, you clean it up. I don't sell food or rent equipment. Use the rubbish bins as marked. Navy showers only. You wet yourself then turn the water off. You soap up, then turn the water on to rinse the water off only. We have limited water here. It's rainwater only, so don't waste it. All clear?"

"Perfectly."

He slid a paper forward and asked me to fill in my details. I began filling my details into the form when I noticed he had already filled the length of stay field. Fourteen nights.

"Uh, we'll only be staying the one night, not fourteen."

"Fourteen's the stay, mate."

"No, we only want one night, this is only just a stopover for us."

"Look, mate, you clearly aren't up on the news. There's a fucking pandemic. The government has ordered a lockdown, starting tonight."

"Yes but…"

"No buts, mate. You know what a lockdown is? You can't move about. You stay in the one place. Here."

"Two weeks?"

"Minimum. It's whatever those bigwigs in government decide."

I frowned, pausing for a moment to think. I did not like the idea of being stuck here with this obnoxious man for two weeks, but what choice did we have? Jane searched the web and this was the only camping facility that allowed pets near us. We were too far from anywhere to drive to a new location at this point.

"I need a decision, pops. I'm closing the gate in an hour and that's it, nobody in or out. So, sign or leave. Make a decision."

I had little choice. I signed. Two weeks. Hopefully it would not be as bad as it currently felt.

3

Margaret was a little peeved I had not consulted her before signing, but she understood. She too was unable to get a signal on her phone, leaving us feeling a little in the dark and isolated. It was strange to think we had not grown up with this technology, yet now in our old age we had grown to become so dependent on it that when it did not work, we felt so ignorant and alone. How did we ever cope when we were young?

I tried the motorhome's radio, but there was nothing but static no matter where I turned the dial. Once we connected to the power from the house, I tried the television set we had in the motorhome as well. I sat for twenty minutes trying to tune it before finally giving up. We were cut off from the outside world.

Our motorhome was bought brand new and had all the modern conveniences. Despite my initial trepidation, it was not cramped inside but rather spacious for two, once you got used to it. It had a four-burner gas stove and oven, a refrigerator, air conditioner, television set with built in DVD player, a toilet and even a shower. The bed, which rolled down from the roof and sat over the dining table, had an innerspring mattress and was much more comfortable than I could have imagined. It was top of the line and about five times more expensive than any car I had ever owned, but absolutely worth it.

The only thing I really had trouble with was getting used to having so few possessions on hand. Sometimes I missed having shelves of books, records, clothes and other knick-knacks at hand, but then, did I really need all of that stuff? How many books could I even read in a year? And Margaret had now converted to an e-reader, with enough disk space to hold hundreds of books in less space than one real book. Our music CD collection now existed on an MP3 player the size of my phone. It was a marvel, yet that too was apparently outdated now according to my daughter.

The more I got used to it, though, the more I started to enjoy the minimalistic lifestyle. I could not imagine going back to that huge crate and unloading all our life's possessions once more. Why did we honestly accrue so much stuff?

The motorhome, too, was easy to set up. Once I had connected the water and power and put chocs under the wheels, there was little else for me to do beyond setting up the annex and fold out chairs. Margaret busied herself unpacking inside and boiling water. We could not trust the rainwater directly from the tanks would be bug free, so we boiled it for insurance and left it to cool for drinking water later.

Maisy remained agitated throughout this whole period. She lay on the ground, facing the dam, her eyes open and watchful. Every now and again she would raise her head and let out a low growl. It was very unlike her.

"Should we go meet our neighbours?" Margaret called from inside as I finished unfolding the outdoor chairs under the annex.

"Sure, may as well. I just hope they are a bit more friendly than the owner."

I turned and put my hand out to help Margaret down the motorhome's stairs.

"Always the gentleman," she remarked.

"Only for you, Hot Lips. How's the knee?"

"Oh, it's ok. I could probably do with the rest though. Maybe staying in one place for a while will do me good."

"Well I'm glad you can find one positive to it."

I took Margaret's arm in mine as we walked. The sun was starting to drop below the line of the ranges to the west as we walked across to the group at the fire. Birds flew overheard, and from up in one of the red gums, a kookaburra called noisily. Maisy trotted alongside us. Her hackles were still raised and her manner was alert like a guard dog. As we closed on the group at the fire, I saw the three people more clearly. A young man and woman of Asian appearance sat close together and appeared to be a couple. The male had a long fringe with blonde tips and a stud earring in one ear. His clothing looked too big for him and was brightly coloured. He had a round face and was a little on the chubby side. The girl at his side had dyed red hair and a broad mouth with a perfect set of white teeth. She smiled regularly as the group talked. She wore tight fitting clothing, accentuating her lean figure, and her hair was in pigtails. She came across as very cute.

As we got closer, the third man in the group stood up and approached us with this hand held out.

"G'day, I'm Chris."

I took his hand and shook it. He had a strong, professional handshake. Chris was a tall man with a muscular frame and broad shoulders. He had blond hair and piercing blue eyes. He had a square jaw and was in need of a shave. His demeanour was warm and friendly, the polar opposite of the owner of the farm.

"This," he said, pointing to the Asian couple, "is Sada and Matsui. They are tourists from Japan."

"Nice to meet you. I am Paul and this is my wife Margaret. And this furry mut is Maisy."

"Hi, it's nice to meet you," the girl said in a thick accent, "would you like some green tea?"

"That would be lovely," answered Margaret.

We went to settle with the group when I realised, stupidly, that we had left our chairs back with the motorhome.

"No worries," said Chris, "I'll go up and get them."

He dashed off energetically in long bounds.

The Japanese girl carefully lifted the kettle that was sitting over the fire and poured the steaming green tea into two mugs. She passed them to us.

"Thanks," I said. "Sorry, but which one were you, Sada or Matsui?"

I felt Margaret pinch my arm and I started to feel the heat in my face redden. Margaret always pinched me when she felt I had said something rude. It was her way of signalling disapproval. It was an honest question, but Margaret must have thought me rude to ask. I had not heard many Japanese names before, how was I to know which was the boy's name and which was the girl's?

"Matsui," she responded with a smile. She then bent over to get closer to Maisy. "Hello there Maisy, may I pat you?"

"Better not," I said, "she's been a little funny today. I think all the travel has made her moody."

Chris returned shortly and set our seats down with the group. Maisy sat close, still alert as she watched the dam. I took a sip of the green tea. I had never tried it before. It was not unpleasant, but not to my taste either.

"Do you like it?" Sada asked.

"Yes, it's nice," I lied. Margaret agreed, and I think she was genuine.

"Before you joined us," Chris started, "we were talking about Australian wildlife. Specifically, kangaroos. I was saying how they spend most of the day lazing about and keeping cool. It's about this time, as it starts to cool off, that they are active. I was expecting to see some coming through here but I've been here two nights now and I haven't seen one."

"We saw a group not far from here as we were driving in," Margaret said.

"See. Now that's weird. They are in the area. There's plenty of plush grass here, I wonder why they don't come on this farm."

I remembered the hunting rifle I saw mounted in the entrance hall of the house. "Maybe the owner hunts them?" I suggested.

At the mention of the owner, Chris eyed me critically. "What did you make of him?"

I cleared my throat and shifted in my chair. Should I tell the truth here? We were stuck here for two weeks and I did not want to be getting off on the wrong foot with the owner or our new neighbours. I glanced at Margaret, who met my eyes and gave a slight shrug.

"We didn't find him to be the friendliest of people," I ventured.

Chris rocked his head back and laughed. "Not friendly? The bloke is a dead set dickhead. He's been rude to every single one of us. You're probably right. He probably shoots at the 'roos and now they stay away from here."

I found myself warming to Chris. He had an affable, friendly manner and was not afraid to call a spade a spade. I appreciated that in a man, even if I was not always that way myself.

Chris took a sip of tea and then asked our story. I gave him a quick rundown on how we had sold our home and set out to travel around Australia. I mentioned our daughter, and her pregnancy with what would be our first grandchild. But I left out the details of how she had stopped talking to me. I did not see it was part of their business.

"That's great," Chris said as I finished telling our story, "I hope one day I can do the same. I'm doing a bit of it now actually. I'm an accountant from Adelaide, but I recently took a voluntary redundancy from my job after my company lost a major contract. I thought I'd take the chance and see a bit of the country and ride to Darwin and back. One of those bucket list things I've always wanted to do. Go and see Uluru, King's Canyon and all of that." He gestured to Sada and Matsui. "These two just came from there."

"Yes, we flew from Japan into Darwin and drove down from there," Matsui said. "We flew over with all our camping gear."

"Wow," said Margaret, "that's quite the ambitious plan. What was your favourite part so far?"

"Well," Matsui continued, "Sada really liked the jumping crocodiles in Kakadu, but my favourite was Uluru."

She had trouble pronouncing the name, and as she said it, it sounded like she had said 'Ururu'.

"I hope you don't mind me asking," I said, "but I noticed your pronunciation of Uluru was off. Why is it Japanese people have trouble saying the letter R?"

Margaret leaned close and I felt a pinch on my arm. Was I being rude? I was genuinely curious, and I'd never met a Japanese person I could ask before.

"I'm sorry for my husband," she said, "he sometimes says things without thinking first."

Matsui blushed and smiled. "It's ok, I've been asked before. In the Japanese language, the L and R sounds are the same. It's one sound to us. Lr."

"Lr," I repeated, trying to make the sound.

"Yes," she giggled, "like that." She pronounced 'like' as 'rike'.

"But I still don't understand how you can't sound out the difference."

Margaret pinched me once more.

"I've heard," Chris cut in, possibly to save the direction of the conversation, "that mouth movements are learnt when we are babies." He leaned forward, like a guru imparting important information to his pupils. "Babies watch their parents' mouths move when they talk and that's how they learn to move their mouths to make the correct sounds. Once our mouth muscles are trained to move a certain way, it's very difficult to make them do something different. It's why some sounds are easy for some people and difficult for others. Their mouths just haven't learnt to make the correct shapes."

"Fascinating," I said. I had more questions, but at the risk of earning more pinches from Margaret, I decided to hold back and made a mental note to look it up sometime in the future.

"So, Uluru," Margaret said, quickly changing the subject, "how did you like that?"

"Beautiful," Matsui said, "but the flies were horrible. They bite really hard."

"I've heard that. Did you get to climb up the rock?" I asked.

"We wanted to, but we didn't want to disrespect the Aboriginal people. We only walked around it. You have never been?"

"No, but Hot Lips and I were planning to as part of this trip."

"Hot Lips?" Matsui laughed.

"Yes," I snorted, "my nickname for Margaret is Hot Lips."

"Why Hot Lips?" She seemed to find the name quite hilarious.

"Did you ever get the television program M*A*S*H in Japan?"

"No," she frowned, confused.

"In the program there was a character called Margaret Houlihan. My Margaret's maiden name, before marrying me, was also Houlihan. The Margaret Houlihan in the show was nicknamed Hot Lips, so I started using it too. Margaret Hot Lips Houlihan. Margaret also used to look quite a bit like the actress who played Hot Lips as well."

Matsui giggled again. She was very cute.

"And what about you, Hot Lips? Do you have a nickname for Paul?"

"Oh, I sometimes call him 'Major'. It would be weird calling him Frank, who was the lover of Hot Lips Houlihan in the television series."

"I always wanted to be called 'Hawkeye'. He was my favourite character."

"Yes, but you're more of a 'Radar' than you are a 'Hawkeye'," she teased.

"Oh ha ha," I said sarcastically, turning back to the others. I could see from their blank faces they had no idea what we were talking about. But I did see Matsui reach for and take Sada's hand. Evidently there was something she saw in us that she wanted for them.

It was getting quite dark now and Margaret must have noticed it too.

"Well," she said, standing, "it was nice meeting you all, but I have a dinner to cook." She passed her empty mug back to Matsui. I looked down at mine. I had barely touched it. I glanced at them, remembering how I had said I liked it, and quickly drank the rest in a couple of quick gulps. Yes, I was certain now. I did not like green tea. I would have to work out a way of politely declining in the future. I passed my now empty mug back as well and turned to pick up my seat.

"Oh no," said Chris, leaping to his feet, "let me."

I let him pick up and fold the seats. I could do it myself. I was not that old, yet. But there was an eagerness to help from Chris that I could not knock back, as though declining the offer would be insulting him.

We said our goodbyes to Sada and Matsui and walked back to our motorhome. As we did so, we passed Chris' motorbike and his unfeasibly small tent. Which made me wonder...

"You came on that bike?"

"Yeah, that's right."

"Do you have enough food to last through lockdown? Bennet told me he doesn't sell any food."

"No, he doesn't. And you're right, I don't have enough food. I spoke to Bennett today on it. He's going to call the authorities in Port Augusta tomorrow to see what we can do. I'm hoping we can get a delivery or have one person go into town."

"But Port Augusta is hours away."

"Yeah, but it's the nearest major town, so fingers crossed."

After Chris had left, we entered the motorhome and Margaret berated me.

"Really Paul, some of those questions you ask."

"What?"

"You know exactly what."

"I was curious, Margaret."

"Well it's those same bloody types of questions that you asked Zheng all the time when Jane started going out with him. He was always on edge around you, you know? And then you had to go and say that bloody stupid..." she choked on her words, turning away from me. She sniffed, and I had no doubt now she was crying.

"Margaret, I've said it a hundred times and I meant it each and every one of them. I'm sorry."

She wiped her eyes and turned back to me. "No bloody use saying it to me."

"Well, you're the only one who listens."

"I just don't understand sometimes why you can't think before you talk. Who cares what our mixed-race baby grandchild will look like? It's still our grandchild."

"I know that Margaret and I don't care. I will love it regardless."

"Then why did you say that remark to Jane and Zheng? They think you're a bloody racist, and sometimes I wonder it myself."

"I'm not a racist, Margaret, you know that. I was just hoping..."

"That the baby wouldn't look too Asian?"

"Margaret, I..."

"No, I don't want to talk anymore and I want to be alone. Go outside and try to calm that dog of yours down. I'll call you when dinner is ready."

Defeated, I left the motorhome and closed the door behind me. Margaret and I were good together for ninety nine percent of the time. Perfect, in fact. We were an excellent match through and through. But that one percent of the time we were not good? Those times were rough. And, sadly, after thirty-five years of strong marriage, that one percent was starting to grow. All for one stupid remark about how my grandchild would look when it came out.

It was a worry. I hoped Jane would forgive me soon, because I doubted Margaret would forgive me until Jane had.

4

I had a lot of trouble sleeping that night.

I replayed again and again in my head that fateful day when Jane and Zheng had stormed out of our home. It was meant to be a joyous occasion. They had flown in from Perth to stay with us and tell us the wonderful news. Instead, thanks to my fat mouth, they stayed in a motel and would only see Margaret. As Cher had once sang, "if I could turn back time".

But it was not just my troubled thoughts that were keeping me awake. It was Maisy too. We kept her in the motorhome at night, sleeping with us. She usually slept under our bed, but not tonight. Tonight, she was restless, constantly pacing back and forth, her toenails clacking against the floor. Often, she would snuff at the door, desperate for a scent of something outside. At one point I thought I heard a gunshot, but the silence that followed made me less certain it was real and not imagined. It was all too distracting and disruptive, and with my thoughts swirling as they were, there was no chance of sleep.

Sometime after midnight I heard the sloshing of water outside. Maisy growled, and started scratching at the door. I shushed her, but she paid no heed of me. She growled a moment longer then stopped. She sat, her ears cropped and her head tilted to the side as though she were listening. I sat up in bed to get a better view. Her behaviour since arriving here had been very odd. She let out a small yap, followed by a small whine. It reminded me of the first time I had tried the dog whistle with her.

The sloshing of water stopped, but curiosity got the best of me and I pushed aside the curtain covering the window to look outside.

At first, I could see very little. The night was cloudy, and very little moonlight was filtering down to light up the farm. My eye was caught by some movement, and I thought I saw a figure dragging something along the ground. I tried to focus on the figure and its bundle, but my eyes could not adjust enough to make anything out clearly.

Maisy growled then barked once more. I turned from the window to shush her. When I turned back, the figure and its burden were gone from sight. I stared a little longer, before closing the curtains again.

It took another two hours before Maisy settled. I had thought in that time I heard more splashing, but between Maisy's scratching at the door and clacking of toenails on the floor, I could not be certain.

It was another two hours after Maisy settled that I finally fell asleep.

When I woke the next morning, I was alone in bed. There were some cold scrambled eggs in a pan on the stove, so I heated those and boiled some water for coffee. Maisy still slept like a log, spread eagled across the floor. She had clearly exhausted herself with all the energy and tension she had in her yesterday. I carefully stepped over Maisy with my plate of warmed eggs and mug of coffee and descended the stairs outside.

Margaret was sitting outside under the annex working on a sudoku puzzle from her book. In recent times she had become quite addicted to sudoku, and spent quite a deal of time with her nose buried deep into the book, working through the puzzles. She greeted me, though not too warmly. Some resentment still remained. I kissed her on the cheek and sat to eat.

The morning was cool but already I could feel the strength of the sun on my skin. The weather was hot here. I would need to take my walks with Maisy in the mornings. Walking was something I did out of enjoyment, but also for health. I was in good shape for a fifty-seven-year-old, and I wanted it to remain that way. My cholesterol levels were borderline, so exercise was important. And Maisy needed it too. She was only four years old, and still a bundle of energy when it came to it. My only regret was Margaret could not join us on the walks. Her knee pained her. It would probably need surgery at some stage. But for now, for this next year, she was comfortable to sit and do her sudoku while I walked with Maisy.

In one of the fields, I spotted Sada and Matsui trying to fly a kite. The day was quite still and bereft of any breeze. They were having little luck. Sada was throwing the kite in the air and Matsui ran holding the string, trying to keep it aloft. Matsui would barely run ten meters before the kite would crash down, dragging along the ground behind her. Despite their failed efforts, the two did seem to be having fun and on more than one occasion I saw them collapse to the ground laughing.

I failed to spot Chris at first, but then I found him jogging back to camp along one of the dusty trails that led up to the ranges to the west. He came into camp, panting heavily, and checked his progress on his watch before doing some warm down stretches.

I watched them all in silence as I ate my breakfast. The eggs were good, and I washed them down with my coffee.

It was as Chris was finishing his stretches that Bennett emerged from his house. He looked like he was wearing the same clothes as yesterday, and already there were fresh sweat stains on his singlet under the armpits. He stomped across the ground in his gumboots and called for us to come to him. He must have an update on the lockdown situation.

I was just about to get up when Margaret told me to stay seated.

"I'll go," she said, "you stay here and finish your breakfast. He won't need both of us."

She dropped her book onto her chair and walked off. I watched her go. Even after thirty-five years of marriage I still had not tired of watching her walk. She just had a way.

I scooped up the last of my eggs then set my plate down. I was too far away to hear anything of the conversation, but halfway through what Bennett said, Chris's body language changed from relaxed to animated and agitated. He crossed his arms and shifted his feet about constantly.

As I downed the last of my coffee, I heard a growl from behind me. Maisy had awoken and had resumed the strange mood that began yesterday. I stood up to shush her, but she looked straight past me. I followed the line of her gaze. She only had eyes for Bennett.

"Easy girl," I said, "I don't like him either, but let's not upset the natives. We are on his land."

She growled again, this time with a greater intensity and with her front teeth bared. I had never seen her this agitated before. I walked towards her, but her eyes remained set on Bennett. I wanted to calm her, so I reached out to pat her head. She must have suddenly become aware of me because she snapped at my hand. I pulled it away just in time, avoiding her vicious bite, before quickly bringing it down again to slap her on the nose.

"Bad girl," I roared.

Something must have clicked in her mind because she suddenly pulled back, a contrite look in her eyes. She had not meant to snap at me, but I told her off anyway. Partly at anger from my fright, partly from the annoyance of her keeping me up all night.

When I turned back, the group had broken up. Margaret was walking back. She frowned slightly. Behind her, Chris, Sada and Matsui talked in a small group while Bennett returned to his house.

"What was that all about?" I asked as Margaret came back.

"That man is disgusting."

"Bennett, I assume?"

"Got it in one."

"What happened?"

"He leered at Matsui the whole time, it was disgusting. He did not look one of us in the eye. I don't know how Sada could stand there and let it happen without saying anything. He's a creep."

I shook my head. I already had a low view of Bennett. This information was not exactly enlightening to hear.

"Ok, but what did he have to say?"

"It's a total lockdown. Bennett says he called through to Port Augusta today. They gave permission for one person only to leave the property. Bennett nominated himself. Now he's the only person who can leave here and go shopping. Anyone else faces a two thousand dollar fine for breaching the lockdown. Can you believe that?"

"Two thousand dollars? Can the government just go and do that?"

"Apparently, they can, and have. They can do it in a state of emergency, which was what they called yesterday."

"How long will it go on?" I was concerned with the effect this would have on our trip.

"Two weeks. Maybe more. It's a bit of wait and see."

I chewed my lip a little. "Ok, I guess we just have to accept that for now. So how will the shopping work then?"

"We will need to make him a list. He'll buy everything we put down and charge us the cost through his credit card machine when he gets back."

I thought on it a moment. It seemed reasonable enough. We probably had enough food on us now to last most of the time, but a little top up would not hurt. Plus, if we conserved the gas for the stove, we should easily get through the next two weeks of lockdown without any food problems. Boredom, however, might be another matter.

"What was Chris' issue?"

"Oh, Bennett said he would only go once today then not again until next week. Chris has nowhere to store the food. He wanted to borrow Bennett's fridge but Bennett refused."

"We could give him space in ours."

"I offered that. I said we'll help where we can but he didn't seem happy."

I felt for him. I really could not understand Bennett. Here was a man who was openly renting his land for people to camp on, yet he did nothing to accommodate his guests and was rude in his manner. No rentals, no equipment and no borrowed space for food. Just land to camp on then leave, plus I'll be brusque to you when we talk and leer at your girlfriends. He must have a terrible rating on the internet.

"I guess we need to make a list then," I offered.

"I'll do it," Margaret said, "you take your walk with Maisy before it gets too hot."

I got the feeling Margaret was still hurt and wanted me to go and leave her alone. It was often her way when we fought. We would have it out, she wanted to be alone and then a day later we were good again. I just needed to give her space. It was one percent of the time, but it had a strict rule I had to follow.

I dropped my dirty dishes in the sink and dressed. I checked I had the dog whistle on me. The way Maisy had behaved yesterday, I wanted to be sure she would not run off. I considered putting her on a lead, but in an open area like this I thought it would be better to let her run. As long as she did not run at Bennett, it would be fine.

I gave Margaret a peck on the cheek before leaving and ushered Maisy to follow me. Maisy was still a little on edge. She would wear herself out again rapidly if she kept this up.

Sada and Matsui had returned to the field and were again trying to get their kite into the sky. Chris was busy trying to stoke the fire back to life. I greeted him.

"Hey Chris, you didn't happen to be out and about late last night, did you?"

"Me? No, I slept like a log. Always have. Why's that?"

"Maisy was pretty restless last night. I could have sworn someone was out here. Oh well, maybe it was Bennett or one of the others. No matter. I saw you jogging earlier, do you know where is a good walking track near here?"

"Yeah, sure. How far do you want to walk?"

"A couple of hours."

Chris stood, brushing his hands together to clean them before turning to point down towards the left of the dam.

"There's a track down there which is quite good. I went down that way yesterday. It winds around to the base of the hill over there before turning back. If you're feeling extra ambitious, there's also a track leading up the hill which gives you an excellent view of the ranges and the surrounding area. If you look east, you'll see Spear Creek itself."

"Great, thanks." I paused a moment, unsure what to say. "Listen, are you alright? You seemed a little animated before."

"Yeah I'm good. It's just I get wound up by that man, Bennett."

"Yeah, he's pretty rude."

"It's like I said yesterday. He's an A-grade dickhead."

I laughed and bid Chris farewell. He certainly was not one to mince his words.

I followed the path he indicated. It was pretty easy to find and follow. I watched Maisy as we walked, careful to monitor her behaviour. As we passed close to the dam, I noticed another change in her. No longer aggressive, she seemed now, if anything, nervous. Her ears were held back, and regularly she glanced towards the muddy waters of the dam. Another curious turn of behaviour. I had not considered it before, but she might have been in heat. Or not. Either way, it was the easiest explanation I could come up with right now.

As the path curved away from the dam, Maisy seemed to recover herself, and soon she was back to her usual, playful four-year-old self. She dashed ahead, running through the grass and chomping at the insects that took flight. After a moment, she stopped and started sniffing at the ground, and her demeanour again changed as the hackles raised on her back. There was long grass to the right of the path, and she disappeared into it. I stopped to wait. I was sure she would be back shortly.

After five minutes, I began to get restless. I called her name. There was no response. I fished the dog whistle from my pocket and gave a quick blast. I could not hear it, but it was on her frequency and she always returned when I blew it. Only this time she did not.

I gave the whistle another blast and called again. There was no movement of grass and I could not hear a thing. I recalled she did this yesterday and returned with blood on her nose. I wondered if she had found, or killed, another animal in the grass. I decided to walk in and investigate.

I called again as I waded through the grass, but still there was no response. Ahead I saw a flattened patch of grass and I made my way towards it. As I did, I noticed some of the blades of grass about me were already bent forward and broken, as though something big had already passed this way. As I approached the flattened grass, I started to hear a buzzing and I noticed the air above the area was thick with flies. There was also a strange, coppery smell to the air.

Ahead, I saw Maisy sitting in the grass, looking at the flattened area.

"Maisy," I called, but she did not respond. Her weird behaviour was starting to really get to me.

I stepped forward and got my first view of what she was looking at.

Upon the flattened grass was the bloodied remains of a kangaroo. It was a big kangaroo too. Its head, paws and tail were intact, but the flesh of its body had been torn away, revealing red stained bones with meat hanging in raw bloody chunks. Its stomach had been completely ripped away, as had the meat from the legs and arms. The empty ribcage revealed all its innards had been removed. Something, or things, had completely torn this kangaroo apart and devoured it. I turned away, gagging.

I took a moment to recover myself, and after taking a sip of water from the bottle I brought with me, I dared one more look at the dead kangaroo. It was an awful mess. Whatever had torn this unfortunate beast apart had literally done so with claws or teeth. I could not imagine what animal could have done this. I was about to turn away again when I noticed something odd. There was a small, round, bloody mark just under the skull. It looked like a bullet hole where the unfortunate kangaroo was shot.

Bullet hole? That made little sense. Unless this dead kangaroo was what the figure I saw last night was dragging along the ground. I was pretty sure I heard a shot too. Now I was certain I had not imagined that. But why kill a kangaroo and leave it here to be eaten by… what exactly?

I felt a shiver run down my spine just as I had when we entered Spear Creek Farm late yesterday. I suddenly no longer felt the urge to walk any more. I stepped forward and pulled Maisy back out of the grass by the collar. She did not resist, and came away easily.

I started to wonder about Maisy's behaviour then. Maybe it was not so odd. Maybe she sensed or smelled whatever animal had done this to the kangaroo corpse.

I decided to return back to camp. I was in a bit of a daze as I walked and failed to notice when Maisy ran ahead to hide under the motorhome.

As I approached the camp, Chris greeted me.

"Back so soon?" he asked.

"Uh, yeah," I responded, still somewhat hazy. "I saw something that destroyed my desire to keep walking."

He looked at me strangely, one eyebrow raised as if asking a question.

"There's a dead 'roo out there in the grass. It had been completely torn apart, inside and out. There was blood everywhere."

"Jesus," Chris cursed. "What could have done that?"

"Dingoes," answered Bennett. I jumped. I had not seen him approach and his sudden presence took me completely by surprise.

"Dingoes?" Chris retorted scornfully. "There aren't any dingoes this far south."

"Yes, there are," Bennett countered, "I've seen them."

"Bullshit."

Bennett stepped forward and pointed his finger aggressively at Chris. There was definitely heat between these two and for a moment I thought a fight may break beyond just an exchange of words.

"It's dingoes, arsehole. They kill the 'roos hereabouts. Happens all the time. As it happens, I heard some growling and barking last night. I thought it was your dog, Paul, but it must have been them dingoes killing that 'roo you saw. Now, I just came down here to let you know I'm leaving for Port Augusta two o'clock. Anything you need, put on a list and have it to me before then."

Without waiting for a response, Bennett turned and walked out to the field where Sada and Matsui continued to play.

"That man..." Chris started.

"I know," I said, slapping him on the back. "Top tier dickhead. Don't let him get to you."

"I'll try," Chris said, "but I can't make you any promises."

5

One of the biggest problems of lockdown, it seemed, was restlessness and boredom. Everything at the farm was plain and idle and, as the day grew longer, the heat became too stifling for physical activity.

I had spent most of the morning (after my aborted walk) tinkering with the radio and television sets in the motorhome, trying to find a signal. After a fruitless hour, I gave up. I could not get anything other than static on either of them.

Getting a signal on our phones was an equally wasted exercise. I spent a good thirty minutes walking around the farm with my phone raised above my head, searching for a bar. I think I may have looked like a comical figure to Sada and Matsui, who giggled when I walked past with my arm stretched high, but I paid them no heed. Chris told me it was futile, he could not even get a signal up on the hill where the ranges were, but I gave it a go nonetheless.

I decided to ask Bennett if he had a computer or WIFI we could access to get news of the outside world and use to communicate with friends and family, but I was given a swift and curt rebuff upon asking. He was evidently able to get news of the world from somewhere, but clearly he was not willing to share it with us.

It was frustrating having no access to any news or information other than what Bennett told us. He was difficult to talk to. What information he did share was sparse and rarely helpful, and he had no patience for questions. And so, we were barely even halfway through day one of lockdown on Spear Creek Farm and already there was a sense of restlessness and isolation.

The sluggishness of the day seemed most telling on Chris. He had made this trip alone with nothing but his motorbike, backpack and tiny tent, which left him with little room for anything else. He tried to keep himself busy with exercise, but the baking sun soon put a stop to that. We offered him books, but he was not a reader. He instead walked circles around the property, thinking who knew what.

At noon, he knocked on our motorhome door to invite us for a rock skimming contest over on the dam. Sada had already accepted, and he wanted to know if we wanted to have a try as well.

"Not for me," Margaret said, "but you go, dear. You've been banging around all morning with the gadgets on this home and distracting me. I need the peace to finish this sudoku."

I decided to go along for the fun of it. It would only fill a short space of time but at least it was something to do. And besides, it seemed it would be good for Chris to have something to do and someone to talk to as well.

The dam was quite large, despite the waterline having dropped a few meters during the heat of summer. It was a typical muddy brown farm dam. Even at the shallowest point, the muddy water was too thick and dirty to see through. There was no telling how deep the dam actually was, but judging from the strict 'no swimming' order issued by Bennett, it must have been quite deep in the middle.

Sada, as it turned out, had never skimmed a rock across water before in his life. Chris, who seemed to relish in the role of a teacher, talked with great energy and enthusiasm.

"First, you need to find the perfect rock," Chris began. "It needs to be flat and round. Here, this is a good one, look at this. Like a discus, you see. Now, you hold the edges between your thumb and forefinger, like this. See? Now when you throw it, it needs to be low, flat and hard, and you need to flick it so it spins. The idea is the flat bottom of the rock skims the water and bounces off it. Watch this."

Chris stepped to the water's edge and bent low. With a quick, flinging action he threw the rock projectile hard and low across the dam. The rock spun, hitting the water and bouncing across its surface. I counted it bounce ten times before tumbling to a stop and sinking into the depths of the dam.

"Nice," I said, "how are we going to measure the contest? Most bounces or longest distance?"

"Most bounces I reckon. Easiest to measure."

We let Sada have a few test throws. His execution was pretty clumsy, and his first few attempts he threw the rock high, causing it to land mid dam with a resounding plonk. Sada did not talk much, but Chris was coaxing him and soon I realised it was not for shyness that he did not talk much, but embarrassment of his English-speaking skills. It made sense now why Matsui did most of the talking last night.

Chris let out a big cheer as Sada got his first stone to skip. It was only three bounces, but the look of achievement on his face was like that of a child. I felt happy for him and cheered as well.

We starting walking along the shoreline, sorting through the various stones we found in preparation for the competition. Maisy joined us at that point. She had that restless look about her again, and regarded the dam suspiciously. I patted her on the head and encouraged her to paddle in the shallows, which I knew she liked, but she suspiciously refused. She began panting, and I was a little surprised she did not want to feel the coolness of the water on her paws and legs.

"Not a bad idea though," said Chris, he sat down next to a pile of skimming rocks he had collected and began stripping off his shoes and socks. He was up again quickly, gathering his small projectiles into his hands before stepping into the water.

"What's it like?"

"Well, let me put it this way. If you like the feeling of slimy mud oozing between your toes, you'll like this."

I did not fancy it, but Sada obviously did and soon he too was sitting on the ground taking off his shoes and socks. Sada stepped into the water not long after and, judging from the look on his face, I took it that the experience was even less glamourous than Chris had made out, if that was at all possible.

"Ok," Chris said, "let's begin. I'll go first."

Chris' first official throw was less effective than his earlier demonstration, measuring just eight bounces as it skipped across the calm dam surface. Sada went second, achieving a score of five on his first throw. It was a massive improvement over his test throws and he was very pleased. I picked amongst the pile I had gathered, looking for my perfect opening gambit. Eight skips should not be too hard to beat. I remembered doing this a lot with Jane when she was young, so I was well practised in the art. I found the right stone. It was a little on the bulky side, and not too flat, but I was pretty confident I could get it to bounce well if I threw it right.

I stepped close to the shore and set myself to throw when Maisy let out a growl. I looked back and her hackles were raised and her teeth bared. Her eyes were set on the muddy water of the dam.

"Easy girl," I said, but she continued to growl.

"Is she normally like that?" asked Sada in his thick accented way.

"No. She's just been acting weird since we got here."

"Don't blame her," Chris added, "there is something off about this place. I've felt it too. You'd better keep an eye on her, she might be sensing whatever killed that 'roo you saw."

"Maybe," I said, though I had already come to the same conclusion earlier myself and I certainly did not believe the dingo story.

Maisy continued to growl, and despite any warning or threat I told her, she would not stop.

"Don't worry about it," Chis said. "As long as she's not going to bite any of us, we can ignore her. Have your go."

I nodded. Whatever had gotten into her was not going away easily and I could not hold up the game any longer. I bent down once more, readying myself. I pulled my arm back, ready to sling shot the rock across the dam.

"Hey," came an aggressive yell from behind me. The momentary distraction caused me to mess up my throw, and the stone went high.

"What the fuck are you idiots doing?" It was Bennett. He was storming across the farm towards us, face red and sweaty. "Get away from the fucking dam, now."

None of us moved, shocked at the extreme reaction to a simple game of rock skimming. Bennett arrived quickly, his eyes wild and his beard carrying flecks of foam and saliva from spitting as he yelled.

"Get out of the fucking water, you idiots. Didn't you hear me say the fucking rules."

Bennett's yelling was drawing attention, and I could see Margaret and Matsui in the distance were now standing and watching the scene. Maisy took two steps towards the dam and continued to growl.

"You said no fishing and no swimming. We're not doing either," I said innocently.

Bennett did not even look at me. He focused on the two standing in the dam water. "Get out," Bennett screamed again, and stepped forward and grabbed at Sada.

Sada tried to push him away, but Bennett grabbed him by the t-shirt and pulled. Sada stumbled to his knees as the fabric on his t-shirt tore. Chris dropped his rocks and lurched forward towards Bennett. The situation was escalating rapidly and I did not like where it was headed, so I too rushed forward. Chris pushed Bennett with two hands square in the chest. Bennett stumbled back a few steps before falling backwards onto his rump. Chris clenched and raised his fist and went to step forward once when I stepped in his path.

Chris glared at me, and I could tell he had been waiting for this excuse to give Bennett a good thumping. I held up my open hands and pleaded for him to stand down. Behind me, Bennett had scrambled back to his feet.

"Yeah," Bennett yelled, "you'd better stand down or I'll fucking kill you, arsehole."

Chris was a bit bigger than Bennett, and had more meat on him as well, so the threat seemed a bit hollow to me. Chris was broad and muscular, and had that look of someone who knew how to scrap. I would back Chris in a fight any time, but I did not want to see this fight eventuate. Not while we were locked down here together, and not while we relied on Bennett to travel to Port Augusta for us.

"Nobody's fighting today," I said in a loud voice. Chris looked at me questioningly, quickly followed by a frown of disappointment. Maisy's growl suddenly peaked in intensity.

"Then you better get away from my fucking dam," Bennett continued to yell. "Now."

"Alright Bennett," I said loudly again, "we're moving away from the dam."

I nodded my head, indicating to Sada he needed to get out of the water. I noticed, then, that a number of ripples were playing on the surface of the dam. I had not noticed when my thrown rock had hit the water, but I must have thrown it high to have caused this many.

Sada and Chris walked up the bank, picking up their shoes in the process.

"You stay away from my fucking dam, got it?" Bennett yelled. He then looked across the water, scanning it for a moment, before turning to leave.

"What was that about?" Chris asked as soon as Bennett had gone out of earshot. "We were just throwing stones."

"I know. It was pretty innocent. He didn't need to go off like that," I answered.

"You should have let me hit him."

"I think I would have liked to have seen it. But it's his property, remember, and so it's his rules. Besides, he's the only one who can leave the farm and go shop for food. If I let you hit him, he could renege on the deal and leave us with nothing to eat."

"True," Chris said, conceding the point. "But it does prove yet again one thing. What is it I always say about him, Sada?"

"World champion dickhead."

Chris laughed and gave Sada a high five.

"Now you're getting it," he said. I smirked. Perhaps there was something in Chris' little game of 'how many ways to say how much of a dickhead Bennett was'. It would not change how he treated us or how we reacted to him. But at least it gave us an outlet and was a nice little way of adding humour to a sticky situation and easing tensions, which was exactly what was needed now.

6

Bennett left the residence at about half past two. There was little formality to it. He said nothing to us, he just drove off without a word. Our only indication he had gone being the cloud of dust his old sedan left in its wake.

His departure was good for us though, taking with it the tension that had been hanging over everyone since the incident by the dam.

The afternoon was achingly hot, and we had the air conditioning in our motorhome turned up to its highest setting just to cope. Chris, with just his small tent, had no real place to shelter from the day's heat, so we invited him in to join us. To avoid being rude, we also invited Sada and Matsui as well, and soon we all sat cramped around our small dinner table inside the motorhome.

Margaret pulled a deck of cards and we began filling our time playing a variety of games. At first, we played rummy, a game that Margaret and I had only recently learnt and enjoyed playing together. I found it equally as fun for five players and it was proving to be a good way to pass the time.

Then Matsui suggested that we learn a Japanese card game called *Daifugō*. I had never heard of it, and as she and Sada tried explaining the rules in their broken English, I started getting very confused. As we played, my confusion only grew worse and at the end of each round I was the '*daihinmin*', which I think meant dunce. For some reason I had to keep giving my best cards away before each round, and kept getting bad ones in return. Matsui was an absolute shark at this game, winning most rounds and remaining the *daifugō*. The game did require constant changing of chairs, which added a great social mixing element, and I found it fun despite my constant last place finishes.

At the end of the fourth round, Matsui said the rules stated that the *daihinmin* was also like a slave and could be sent to get drinks and snacks for the other players. She then told me to get her bottle of water that she left by her tent. At my frown, Margaret gave me a little kick under the table and soon I was back out under the baking sun.

I walked over to Sada and Matsui's campsite and found their drink bottles with ease. The water inside felt hot, but we had room in our refrigerator and could cool it off. As I turned back to our motorhome, I noticed that in Bennett's haste, he had left the door of the shed open. I was curious, and I was sure the others could wait a little longer for their *daihinmin* to return, so I decided to investigate.

The shed was old, but had been recently repainted green to belie its age. The paint job was patchy. Clearly not the work of a professional. The shed itself was mainly made from thin sheet metal, and where it had not been freshly painted, there were clear signs of rust. I pushed aside the main door, the metalwork groaning as it moved. The inside of the shed was quite dark, but the sunlight punctured the darkness through various holes in the walls and roof. I examined one of the holes more closely. It was a round hole, looking very much like a puncture mark with the inside revealing shards splayed outwards. I was not a forensic expert, but they did look remarkably like bullet holes.

As my eyes adjusted to the light inside, I deduced that this had once been a bustling shearing shed. The inside of the shed itself was separated into many parts by wooden barriers and gates. These formed various holding pens and races to guide the sheep about. At the centre was the main shearing area. On the wall hung great, scissor like objects, strung up as though on display in a museum as relics from shearing days long past. The farm had since modernised, as in the centre pen, electric shears hung down from cables from the roof. This had been a long-used shearing shed, possibly dating back a hundred years.

I put Sada and Matsui's drink bottles down and clambered over the barriers, making my way to the centre pen. There was an odd odour here, like old mothballs, and there was still clumps of old wool on the floor. I reached up and unhooked one of the shears from the post. I turned it over in my hand. The blades still shone. I flicked the switch on and it buzzed to life. I quickly turned it off again, worried of being caught trespassing, even though I knew Bennett was gone.

I wondered how long this sheep station had been out of use, replaced by what was now a campground. The house had also looked quite old, and this farm was probably like many in the area: passed down from generation to generation. What had stopped it? A fool like Bennett no doubt. He was probably the last in line. The failed farmer.

I carefully replaced the shear back up on its hook and left the shearing shed. It was sad to think that this farm was probably passed down from father to son multiple times before Bennett had destroyed its livelihood. It was a beautiful area and a stunning piece of land. I tried imaging the place in its prime as a thriving sheep station.

Stepping back out into the sun, I closed the shed door behind me. The venture in the shed had got me curious though, so I walked around to the sliding door entrance to the farm house. I tried it. It was unlocked. I checked my watch. Bennett had been gone two and a half hours. I looked up the driveway. There was no sign of him. I opened the door and went in.

The house was hot inside and the air tasted stale. The office was the same as yesterday. The counter was still strewn with paper. I walked over and examined them. They were the same forms I had filled yesterday. I peered over the counter to see a box filled with even more forms. I walked around the counter to look at them more closely. On the top of the pile was my form which I had signed yesterday. Underneath that, a second bearing the names Sada Koji and Matsui Mai. Under that, Chris McEwen. Evidently Bennett's filing system was as good as his farming.

I checked at the next form. It was a form for a man named Jay Rahaley. I looked at the date. Three days before Chris had checked in, and Jay had also signed for a fourteen day stay. I frowned. What had happened to Jay? Perhaps he was not able to handle staying with Bennett and left early? It was not hard to imagine. I flipped the page over. There was nothing noted there.

I returned the paper to the box and stood up. I was not sure this was helping, but I did remain curious. Aside from the doorway covered by the bead curtain, there was another door at the opposite end of the room partly obscured by posters. I ignored this door and instead pushed my way through the bead curtain into a short hallway. A couple of empty, crushed beer cans lay on the floor. The carpet was well worn and coming up around the edges. It was badly frayed in some spots. There was also great clumps of dirt and grit. I doubted it had been vacuumed in months. There were two doors to the right and one at the end of the hall.

I walked down the hall and peered through the first door. The room was cluttered with all manner of objects creating a huge mess. There was camping gear, balls, toys, books, magazines and all sorts of objects, all seemingly thrown in here at random. It looked like an assortment of objects other campers must have left behind, but there was no order to the collection. The curtains were drawn tight, and I wondered why Bennett chose to hide these objects and not make them available for other campers to use.

The next door led into a bathroom. There was a toilet and shower here, though both were filthy. The floor of the shower was stained black, and the open toilet bore stains of its most recent use. This was not a room I wanted to loiter in.

The door at the end of the hall led to a bedroom. A double bed, with an elaborate, steel framed headboard, stood against the back wall. There was just a top sheet on the bed, and it was stained brown with sweat and dirt. There were numerous empty, crushed beer cans all over the floor. Facing the bed, next to the doorway, was a tallboy dresser. Sitting on top of the dresser was a small television set and DVD player. The top drawer of the dresser was slightly open, revealing an extensive pornographic DVD collection within. From the few covers I saw, he seemed to have an Asian fetish.

It was close now to five o'clock and I was considering switching on the television set to see if I could catch some news when I heard the sound of an engine and the crackling of gravel outside. I stepped over to the window, pushing the curtain aside to see Bennett's car pulling up beside the house.

My heartrate leapt and I began to panic. I did not want Bennett to find me snooping around his house. I quickly pulled back from the curtain and stepped towards the door. I had not seen another door out so I would have to try and sneak out the front way. As I crossed the room, I stepped on a discarded beer can. It curled up and stuck to my shoe.

I walked down the hallway with the can still stuck on my shoe. It crinkled with each step, but Bennett was outside and unlikely to hear. Besides, I needed to get out the front door before he saw me or, at worst, be found in the entrance looking at the pictures on the walls. I pushed through the bead curtain and past the counter. Bennett had pulled his car to a stop just in front of the glass sliding door of the office. I crept up to the glass door and peered out. I could see through the car window. Bennett was fiddling with something in his middle console.

I slowly lifted my foot and pulled the can free. I dropped it carefully behind the counter. It landed on a box and made no noise.

I heard the car door open and close. I froze for a moment, expecting at any instant for Bennett to open the door. A few seconds passed and I heard Bennett's footsteps receding. I darted forward and dared a look through the glass door. Bennett was walking towards our motorhome. He must have deduced we were all there.

His back was to me, so I carefully slid the door open. It was thankfully whisper quiet, and soon I was outside and closing the door again behind me. I could see on the back seat of the sedan the grocery bags sitting on two slabs of beer. I suddenly felt like I needed a stiff drink myself.

Bennett was knocking on the door of our motorhome now. I was still in the open and exposed. I looked around quickly. There was nowhere to hide, so I dashed around to the side of the house and behind the water tanks.

I stopped a moment behind them, breathing heavily. My heart was racing and I needed a moment to catch my breath. Sweat was thick on my brow and I wiped it away. I took a couple of deep breaths to calm myself. I started to feel better when I realised I would be found soon and I needed to have a reason for being here.

The area behind the house was more fields and red gums. There was no reason for me to be out there. I had nothing. I would have to wing it.

When I felt ready, I walked around the house again. Bennett was returning from the motorhome. His brow crinkled as he regarded me suspiciously.

"What were you doing back there?" he asked, not even bothering to cover the hostility in his voice.

"Uh," I stuttered, "looking for my dog."

He scrunched his face up. "It's under your van, you idiot."

I looked, and even from this far away, Maisy was clearly visible under the motorhome.

"Ah," I said, "So she is."

Without saying more, I walked back towards the motorhome. As we crossed paths, Bennett reached out and grabbed my arm. He pulled his face close to mine, and he had the stench of alcohol on his breath.

"I'm getting' sick of that bitch dog growling at me."

I smiled disarmingly. "Not much I can do about that."

"Just keep it tied. If I see that dog running around where it shouldn't, I'll shoot the bitch. Got it?"

He did not wait for my answer but pushed me away. I was tempted to turn and smack him, but I was long past my prize fighting days, so I walked on towards our motorhome. I was sure I could sense his stare at my back as I walked. I tried to look as nonchalant as I could, even if I did not feel it. My legs felt like jelly.

Back at the motorhome, I gave Maisy a quick greeting before stepping inside.

"Where have you been?" asked Margaret, a slight tinge of concern to her voice.

"We were worried you got lost," added Chris.

I gave them a sheepish smile. I wondered if they had peeked through the windows and watched me while I was snooping around.

"And where is my drink bottle, *daihinmin?*"

The drink bottles! I put them down... where?

Shit.

7

Bennett had taken all of our groceries inside while he sorted whose items belonged to whom, and how much money we all owed him.

Sada and Matsui were not too bothered about their lost water bottles, but I was. I had left them behind, exploring somewhere I should not be, and forgotten where I placed them. What if Bennett found them? Would he conclude someone had been snooping around? And how would he react if he did? These thoughts worried me.

The lust for the card game had died down with Bennett's return, and Margaret packed them away while we waited. It was amazing how one man's presence could dampen our small group's mood so much, but Bennett had that effect. Even when he was not in the room.

We did not have to wait long for him to come from his house and call for Sada and Matsui. Once they had gone, Margaret sought to break the silence first.

"What did you get him to buy for you, Chris?" she asked.

"Oh, mostly canned stuff that I can just open, heat and eat over the fire. It's not healthy, but I can deal with it for a couple of weeks if I need to. It made sense. I need non-perishables that I can keep in the tent. Beans, spaghetti... that sort of suff."

"You didn't need to get that. We could have stored your food for you."

"In that little fridge? Nah, don't worry about it, Margaret, I'm good. Besides, I bought some beer as well, I was hoping you'd keep that cool for me."

Margaret frowned. "Hmm," she grumbled, "it seems you have the same sense of priorities my Paul here has. Beer. Hmpf."

"So, you bought beer too then?"

"No, we didn't," Margaret said.

Chris gave me a funny look so I decided to explain.

"On our way to Adelaide," I said, "we went through a number of wine regions. We bought quite a few bottles, and we're slowly working our way through them. We have a fair variety, so we are giving them all a go. We're keeping scores too, so when we come back through this way later on, we know which ones to get again. Speaking of which, what do you feel like drinking tonight, Hot Lips?"

"Already a step ahead of you there, Major. I have a McLaren Vale Chardonnay already in the fridge chilling for later."

"Nice."

Chris gave me a weird, warm, knowing smile then.

"What?" I asked.

"You two," he laughed. "I most definitely am going to do this when I'm your age."

I did not quite follow what he meant but I took it as a compliment.

Suddenly we heard shouting outside from the farmhouse and Maisy barked loudly. Chris and I shot up from our seats and were quickly outside. By the farmhouse, Bennett and Sada were having a terse exchange. Sada had struck me as quite mild mannered to date, and seeing him this animated was quite a shock. Matsui was trying to pull Sada away from the argument, which eventually he reluctantly did. The move, though, only caused more problems as Sada, obviously not satisfied with the outcome, turned his frustrations over to Matsui and they began their own little private squabble.

Bennett, a smug look plastered over his face, then called for Margaret and I to come over.

I have to admit I did feel a bit nervous about confronting Bennett again. I reached for Margaret's hand as she came down the steps of the motorhome and continued to hold on as we walked across the space between our motorhome and the farmhouse. Holding Margaret's hand always helped me feel stronger than I actually was.

In the office, Bennett had placed our bags of groceries on the counter. Bennett was his typically unfriendly self, not even bothering to acknowledge us as we entered. We checked over our inventory. Bread, pasta, soups, cereal, vegetables, long-life milk and sauces, not one of them being the brand we requested. No meat and, unsurprisingly, no toilet paper. Evidently that shortage remained in place.

"No newspaper?" I asked.

"Sold out."

Damn, I had been hoping to get more news of the outside world.

"Ok, so how much do we owe you?"

"That'll be two hundred and fifty bucks," Bennett drawled.

I blinked, trying to keep my reaction from showing on my face.

"Two hundred and fifty dollars? For this?"

My voice must have revealed my incredulity, because he looked at me sharply.

"That's what I said, old man. Two hundred and fifty bucks. Now how are you paying?"

"But this haul shouldn't even cost more than eighty dollars."

Bennett continued to stare at me hard. "Prices have changed. Call it a pandemic adjustment. Everyone is stocking up on shit now the whole world has come to a stop. This is the price now. Two hundred and fifty bucks."

This was outrageous. But could it be true? Had the shutdown caused so much to stop so quickly that prices skyrocketed so quickly? Surely even supermarkets in a small town like Port Augusta kept enough reserve stock on hand that it would not come to this? And what would the consumer watchdog say about it if the supermarkets were doing this?

Then I almost slapped myself. Of course, it was not the supermarkets. How could I be so stupid to think that first?

"Can I see the receipts?" I asked.

"No, you can't. Two hundred and fifty is the price. It's non-negotiable. Now pay up or fuck off."

"You're lying, Bennett. You're ripping us off."

Bennett made an over exaggerated sigh, rolling his eyes and clutching at his heart with two hands. Then he laughed. It was a clearly fake laugh, and he leant forward, close to my face as he gave the last few exaggerated ha's. Again, I was struck by the rank alcohol stench of his breath. I glared at him, but the effect seemed to only amuse him. He was taking advantage of us openly, and he did not care that we knew it. In fact, I think us knowing only made him enjoy it even more.

"We'll pay by credit card," Margaret said.

I gave her a sharp look. I felt as if she had suddenly betrayed me.

"We can't pay this price," I said, aghast.

"We can," she said, pulling her hand away from mine. "Give him your credit card."

I wanted to argue the point further but she gave me a sharp look back that told me not to try it. Numbly, I pulled my wallet from my back pocket and fished out my credit card. Bennett took it from me gleefully. Shark grins were warmer than his. I watched in a daze as he processed the booking. I could not believe Margaret did not back me, we should have fought.

Like a zombie, I took my card back and took the groceries from the counter.

"Tell that other arsehole he can come in now," Bennett called over our backs as we left his home.

When we were far enough away, I turned to Margaret and stopped her to talk.

"Why did you do that?" I asked.

"We can afford it, Paul."

That much was true. After the sale of our home, we had far more money than we needed right now sitting in the bank, earning minimal interest.

"That really wasn't the point."

"What was the point, Paul?"

"It's the principle of the thing. He can't just rip us off like that."

She placed her hand on my arm and held it just below the shoulder. A placating gesture she often did when she wanted me to calm down.

"We don't really have a choice here, Paul. He's the only one allowed out, and if he adds a, let's call it a courier fee, so be it. I'd much rather just pay more and keep the peace than start another fight. It's already too tense around here and it's only day one of our lockdown."

I did not want to let it go, and it must have shown on my face.

"Please, Paul. Let it go. Would you rather be like them right now?"

She nodded towards Sada and Matsui. Sada was pacing back and forth, waving his hands wildly and spouting rhetoric angrily in Japanese. Matsui stood still, arms crossed, getting very few words in. Her face was red and her features sadly contorted. I turned back to Margaret.

"No, I don't want to be fighting with you, Hot Lips. I never do, you know that."

"Then let it go. Money is not an issue. There is enough tension around here already, we don't need to add to it."

"Yeah, I know. But Bennett..."

"Yes, it's Bennett. It's all Bennett. All of it. But Paul, let it go please."

I nodded. I hated fighting with Margaret. Mostly because she was always right, and she always won. She was the sensible one in our relationship. All she needed to do was win me over with her logic.

She leaned forward to take the bags from my hands.

"No, I'll carry them," I said.

"No, I will take them, Paul. I want you to do me a favour and stand by the door when Chris goes in. You saw the way Sada and you reacted. I think Chris is a bit of a hot head. You saw that incident by the dam earlier today. He's just itching for a reason to hit Bennett. There's no telling how he'll react when Bennett rips him off too. I'd like you to wait by and make sure World War Three doesn't break out in there."

She had a point, and as much as I did not want to play the role of UN Peacekeeper, it was something this farm needed right now. I let her take the groceries away.

Chris approached with a broad grin on his face as he rubbed his hands together.

"I'm looking forward to getting those beers chilled."

He gave me a chummy slap on the shoulder as he passed me. I turned and slowly followed as he went inside. I wondered how long that positive mood would last as I waited not far from the door. Chris had left the sliding door slightly open, so I would hear any yelling from the room as soon as it started. I expected at any second I would be needed.

Two minutes passed without yelling. I began to worry, when Chris reappeared at the door. He carried a slab of beer on one shoulder and two heavy, can laden bags in the other hand. The weight seemed no bother for him. He was shaking his head, but he wore a grin on his face. He seemed surprised to see me.

"What are you doing here, mate?"

"Margaret asked me to stand by. She was worried about how you would react."

Chris gave a soft chuckle. "I'll be honest. I totally expected that."

"You did?"

"Oh yeah. It follows with what I've always said about him."

"Wait, let me guess. Executive level dickhead."

"Oh no, much higher than that."

"CEO level dickhead?"

"Mate, he sits on the board of directors," Chris chuckled.

It was good to see him act with such humour. Margaret's expected crisis was averted. At least for now.

8

"You never said, where did you disappear to earlier today?" Margaret asked.

Margaret and I were alone in our motorhome preparing our dinner. She stood at the stove, stirring the boiling water to move the pasta around. I was cutting the last of the tomatoes for the sauce. We were using the last of our minced meat, but we both wanted to have a nice meal of spaghetti bolognese tonight. After dinner, we promised to meet the others out by the fire to enjoy a few drinks.

"I... I went exploring."

"Exploring? What, out in the paddocks or something?"

"No, I went into the house."

She stopped stirring, turning to me with incredulous eyes. "What, inside Bennett's house?"

I felt the heat flush to my face and I knew I was reddening. "Yes, Bennett's house."

"Oh my God, why did you do that? What if he had caught you?"

"He almost did," I conceded, remembering how close it had been. I continued to cut the tomatoes but I could feel her staring at me.

"Well?"

"Well what?"

"What was it like? You can't just leave it like that, you have to tell me."

I almost shivered as I recalled. "An absolute pigsty. I think I need a tetanus booster shot just for going in. He had crap everywhere. It looked like it hadn't been cleaned in years. Picture your worst cleaning nightmare. It was like that. One room could easily have been an episode of 'Hoarders'."

"Sounds putrid, but somehow I'm not surprised. He looks like he's been wearing the same clothes for weeks. And that body odour... ugh."

She turned back to the boiling pot and resumed stirring. I stood and tipped the freshly cut tomatoes into the bubbling sauce on the stove before turning the heat down a little.

"Sada and Matsui's bottles. Where did you leave those? Not in the house I hope."

"I... I really don't remember."

"Jesus, Paul. What if he finds them?"

"I don't know."

"You can't let them take the fall for that. If Bennett finds them, you have to admit it was you. Got it?"

I frowned and nodded. Why did I even go in there? It was stupid of me, but I was curious. How did the old saying go? Curiosity killed the cat? Let's hope not.

Margaret started chewing her lip as she stirred. I knew that gesture. It meant she had something she wanted to ask, but she was afraid to do so. A curly question was coming.

"What?" I nudged. "What are you thinking?"

She sighed and turned to me once more. I could see from her face she had a feeling of guilt about what she was about to ask.

"When you were snooping through Bennett's house," she began, "did you happen to see a computer or phone or anything?"

"A computer?"

"Yes. I was hoping to get in touch with Jane. Send an email. I want to let her know we got here OK but we're stuck in lockdown for the time being. Just so she knows."

"No, I didn't see anything of the sort."

I frowned. It only now struck me as odd I had not seen a telephone. There was not one in the office, nor in the rest of the house either.

"You said Jane called through before we got here? Was it a land line?"

"No, mobile I think."

"That's strange. How does he get a signal?"

Margaret shrugged, and the question hung in the air unanswered.

We ate a quiet dinner. Both of us, it seemed, were lost in our thoughts. At around eight o'clock, we fed Maisy. Since Bennett's warning I had kept her on a lead tied to the motorhome. I was not sure how serious Bennett's threat had truly been, but I did not want to tempt fate. Not with him.

At around nine o'clock, we left the motorhome. Margaret brought the wine and I was carrying our fold up chairs down to sit with the others by the fire. I unfolded them and set them down, attaching Maisy's lead to my chair. She settled down beside me, padding at the imaginary grass before lying down. It cooled off very quickly in the night here, and they had already stoked up quite a fire. Margaret brought the drinks, our wine with a couple of plastic cups and a cold six pack of Chris' beer. Chris took his beer gleefully, pulled a stubby from the packet and pressed it against his cheek.

"Ooh yeah, perfect temperature. Many thanks." He opened one and, raising it to his lips, drank half the bottle in one go. "Ah, that's the good stuff." He pulled a second bottle from the packaging and passed it towards Sada. "Here, Sada, have a taste of this. It's a local brew. It's dry, a bit like Asahi. I reckon you'd like it."

Sada took the beer and opened it. He took a quick mouthful and gave Chris a thumbs up.

"Matsui," Margaret said, "I've been meaning to ask you and Sada, how long were you going to stay in Australia?"

"Only one more month. We already have our flights back to Japan booked. As long as the lockdown isn't too long, we will be ok. But I'm a little sad, we may have to miss out on some of the places we wanted to visit."

"I really wanted to visit Kangaroo Island," Sada added.

"Probably worth skipping for now," Chris cut in, "it was pretty devasted by recent bushfires."

And so the conversation turned to bushfires, to Australian wildlife, to traveling and then took a strange right hand turn into times we had broken the law. It was funny the flow of conversations at times, how they could go from normal to outrageous very quickly. I sipped my McLaren Vale Chardonnay. It had a hint of apple, but it was too dry for my taste. I was starting to feel drowsy from the alcohol and lack of sleep from the night before. My head began to nod as I slowly drifted off.

"Bullshit," Chris blurted and I suddenly came back to wakefulness.

"No, it's true," Sada said.

"You got fined by the police for driving through a puddle and splashing a pedestrian? That's insane," Chris laughed.

"In Japan, you are supposed to drive slowly in the rain."

"How much was the fine?"

"I think it was the equivalent of eighty Australian dollars."

Chris clapped his hands and rocked his head back with laughter. There were four empty beer bottles at his feet. How long had I slept? I checked my watch. It was now five minutes to eleven o'clock. The fire was low and the wine in my cup was warm when I drank it.

Margaret saw me come to wakefulness and put her hand on my arm.

"Did you want to go back to bed now?" she asked, smiling warmly.

I finished my wine and rubbed my eyes. I was slowly coming back to life again.

"No, I'm awake now. Let's stay a little longer." I looked across the group. "Where's Matsui?"

"She went to bed already. She's not very good with alcohol," Sada explained. "Would you like to try some sake? It is a Japanese rice wine."

Sada poured a little into a shot glass and passed it across to me. I downed it in one shot. The taste was quite different from anything I had tried before, and not too unpleasant.

"Like it?" Sada asked.

"Nice."

"Would you like more?"

"Ah, how much more wine do we have, Hot Lips?"

"About a quarter of a bottle."

"I might stick with that first Sada, if that's ok?"

"No problem, just let me know."

I poured myself another cup of wine. I took another sip from the cup. Definitely too dry. This one was not getting a repeat purchase on the return journey.

"Have you seen any Drop Bears since you've been in Australia?" Chris asked.

"Drop bears?" Sada asked, a confused look on his face.

I smiled and turned away. What good was meeting a tourist if you could not stir them up about Drop Bears? Chris was such a typical Aussie.

I reached out to Margaret and took her hand. It had become a pleasant night. A little cool, but sitting by the fire sipping on wine and enjoying Chris' enthusiastic re-telling of the Drop Bear story was both warming and relaxing. It was the most enjoyable moment I had had since arriving at Spear Creek Farm.

"That's not true," Sada declared when Chris had finished.

"It is true. Drop Bears are real. Didn't you hear about that torn up kangaroo Paul found earlier today? You know what did that? Drop Bears."

"Torn up kangaroo?" Margaret asked softly. I had neglected to tell her about that.

"Yes, Maisy found it. It was a real mess."

"You should have told me."

"Oh, I'm sure it's nothing that will bother us."

"Maybe so, but if I had known there were dangerous animals about, I wouldn't have let Maisy off her lead."

I sat up quickly and looked down at the empty lead, still attached to my chair.

"Jesus Margaret, it's not the animals we need to worry about. Bennett threatened to shoot her."

Margaret gave me a look, and I realised then that was two important things that I had failed to mention to her. I stood up and looked around. My eyes failed to penetrate far into the darkness. I could not see her anywhere.

"Maisy," I called out. "Maaaaiiiiiiisssssyyyy."

Chris had stopped talking and looked around too now. There was silence, and we all waited. I called again. Nothing.

I felt around in my pockets. I did not have the dog whistle with me, it must be back in the motorhome.

"Keep calling," I said, "I'm going back to the motorhome to get her whistle and a torch. She's probably gone back to that dead 'roo."

All three of them started shouting her name as I left. Inside the motorhome, I found the whistle quickly. The torch was not where it was supposed to be and I spent a couple of wasted minutes looking for it. I tested it, then wasted another couple of minutes searching for replacement batteries. By the time I left the motorhome, I was already more than a little frustrated.

Margaret shook her head as I returned. There was still no sign of Maisy.

I called her name once more. I was starting to feel desperate now. I had a dreadful feeling something was wrong. Something terrible had torn up that kangaroo, and between that mystery and Bennett's threats, I was terribly worried.

"Hey," came a yell from behind me. "What the fuck are you all still doing up? Curfew is at eleven."

Bennett. Shit.

"You lot need to get into you beds, now."

"We need to look for their dog. She's run off," Chris cut in.

Bennett turned to me with his weaselly eyes. "I warned you, mate. I'll shoot that little bitch if she comes near me."

"She won't," said Margaret. "She's not an aggressive dog. She's just a bit uneased by her new surroundings."

His greasy little eyes swivelled to Margaret. "Well I am sure she'll turn up. Right now, it's curfew and you lot need to get in bed. Now move."

"Whoah, hold on," said Chris, "it's only eleven, we need to see if we can find their dog."

Weasel eyes turned to Chris. "You can look around all you want in the morning. Right now, it's curfew, so get moving into your beds."

"Does it really matter if we stay up a little later and look?"

"Yeah it does, now start moving or I'll make you."

"Make us what?"

Chris took an aggressive step forwards towards Bennett. His jaw was set and his fists clenched. There was no doubting his intent. It looked like he was ready to launch toward Bennett when Margaret then stepped between them, facing Chris.

"It's alright, Chris. We can look tomorrow morning, like he said, if she hasn't come back already. She's a smart dog. She'll probably find her way back on her own."

Chris regarded her a moment. He seemed disappointed. Whether it was disappointment that we chose not to find Maisy or disappointment he could not continue to fight, I could not say.

"If that's what you choose."

"It's what I choose."

Chris nodded, but he was clearly dissatisfied with the outcome. He turned back to the fire and set about picking up his empty bottles.

"Just leave those there," Bennett said, his voice slightly higher than normal. Chris looked back at him questioningly. "You can clean it up tomorrow. Right now, it's curfew, just go to bed quickly and sleep."

Chris looked at Bennett a little longer before dropping the bottles and moving on.

"What about the fire?" Sada asked.

"I'll take care of it," Bennett said, "just go."

Sada too, turned.

"Can I at least blow on my dog whistle? It won't make any noise. Well, not on a frequency we can hear at least."

Bennett turned to me, wide eyed.

"No," he barked, "definitely not. You need to go to bed now."

I wanted to stay and argue the point but Margaret looped her arm through mine and pulled me away. I let her lead me a few steps before leaning close to whisper.

"I don't want to go. I want to look for Maisy."

"We need to keep the peace, Paul. It's getting way too volatile."

"I know, but Maisy…"

"It's ok, Paul. He's bluffing. He won't shoot her. And it's like I said to them. She's a smart girl, she'll find her way back. She'll be under the motorhome when we wake in the morning. You'll see."

I had my doubts, and the memory of the torn-up kangaroo corpse hung heavily on my mind.

9

I had planned to stay awake. As we prepared for bed, I formulated the plan in my mind. I would lie in bed beside Margaret and wait for her to fall asleep. I often had problems sleeping, it should not be too difficult for me. Then, once I was satisfied she was in a deep enough sleep, I would get up and sneak out of the motorhome to look for Maisy. I made sure I kept the torch and dog whistle easily within reach, and my shoes by the door, as I prepared for bed. I was ready. I just needed to get out quietly.

Once outside, I would use the dog whistle only and the torch. I could do it all so quietly that no one, not even Bennett, would be aware that I had gone out.

At least that was the plan.

Perhaps it was the wine. Perhaps it was the lack of sleep the night previous to this one. Whatever it was, it did not make a difference as the end result was the same. Sleep. I dropped off quickly not long after getting into bed, much the same as when I sat by the fire.

By the time I woke up, the sun had already crept well up the eastern horizon and the motorhome had begun to heat up. I sat up, half expecting Maisy to be curled up at the foot of the bed on the floor. Only she wasn't.

Margaret still dozed softly as I pulled myself out of bed. I had a slight nagging headache and my mind felt full of cobwebs. My mouth was dry and felt like I had slept with a sock in it. I grabbed the dog whistle from the place I secluded it and walked to the door. My body was somewhat resistant to the plan, but I was getting moving. I needed to find Maisy.

The first place I looked was under the motorhome. It pained me to bend over so far, and I had to stand a few moments after straightening, but I was not going to let my body win over. She was not there.

Chris and Sada were stocking up the fire in preparation to cook breakfast. My own stomach felt queasy as I approached, but I ignored it. I was on a mission. I was too worried about Maisy to worry about trivial things like food.

"Have you seen Maisy anywhere this morning?" I asked, hearing my own desperation in my voice.

"No, not at all," Chris answered. Sada shook his head.

I did a three-hundred-and-sixty-degree turn, shouting her name every few seconds. Nothing. I gave the dog whistle a couple of blasts. Still nothing.

"I'm sure she's alright," Chris added unhelpfully. "Have you checked over by that dead 'roo you saw yet?"

I had thought of it, and also dreaded it. What if I found Maisy there, eating the thing? Or worse, what if she were torn to shreds herself? I was not sure I could handle that, but I realised I could not put it off any longer.

I strode down past the dam and along the track. Sweat started to prickle my brow as I walked, and it was not entirely due to the heat.

It was not easy, but I found the spot on the path where Maisy had run off quite quickly. I paused a moment, gathering myself. My mouth still felt dry, and I wished I had brought some water with me. I took a couple of deep breaths. I was delaying the inevitable, I knew it. I had to go. I took one more breath and started cutting my way through the grass.

I smelled the dead kangaroo long before I saw it. The smell was even worse than yesterday. It should not have come as a surprise, really. A whole day under the baking sun would do that. I pulled my t-shirt up over my nose to hide the smell, but it was little use. In the end, I pinched my nose between my thumb and forefinger to block my nostrils altogether.

The air ahead swarmed thick with flies. Fat, bulbous black bastards buzzing lazily back and forth, gorged on kangaroo meat. I swatted at them, knocking them off their flight paths but doing little to scatter them.

Finally, I stepped onto the flattened grass area. It was a hive of activity. An army of bugs crawled over the red meat mess that was once one of Australia's most beautiful marsupial animals. The eyes had been eaten away since I last saw the body, as had a lot of the meat that had remained on the bones. The bugs had made solid progress on the corpse in just one day. But aside from the bloody mess and swarming insects, there was nothing else here. And most importantly, there was no sign of Maisy.

I stepped away from the bloody chaos and ran back to the path, gasping at the air. As I reached the path I stumbled and dropped to my knees just in time as my stomach upended itself. I wretched maybe three or four times. The vomit was mainly the last remnants of last night's wine and my stomach acids. I felt sorry for the flies. There was nothing chunky in my vomit to drag those bugs away from their meat bounty.

I wiped my mouth with the back of my hand and groaned. Not only was the inside of my mouth feeling dry, I now had the scalding sensation of stomach acid burning the back of my throat. Good times.

I staggered back to my feet and decided to head back to the motorhome. My head still ached and I felt a little dizzy, but I did not think I would vomit again. I walked slowly on the path and as I got back to the camping area, I saw Matsui emerge, graven faced from her tent. She looked like how I felt.

My eyes drifted across the campsite, searching, before finally landing on the farmhouse. Bennett. He probably had something to do with this. With Maisy's disappearance. The arsehole probably did something to her. Maybe even shot her, as he had threatened. I decided I needed to confront him. Now.

I stumbled towards the farmhouse. I think Chris or Sada said something. I was not sure. I was too focused on the farmhouse. On confronting Bennett.

I reached the sliding door and pulled on it. This time it was locked. Frustrated, I started banging on the glass and shouting.

"Get out here Bennett, you bastard," I yelled. "Get out here now."

I saw through the sliding door Bennett stumble through the bead curtain. That hateful man with his stupid haircut and pathetic beard. His stinking clothes and his horrid alcohol breath.

"Get out here," I shouted again.

He gave half a smile and walked to the door, unlocking it. I did not even wait for him. I grabbed the handle and wrenched the sliding door aside.

"Where is she? What have you done to her?"

"What are you talking about, old man?"

"My dog," I screamed. "Where is my bloody dog?"

"I don't know, man."

I started jabbing him in the chest with my finger.

"You know. You did something to her. I know it."

He was not taking it. He shoved me hard in the chest with two hands. I stumbled back a few steps but did not fall. He stepped forward through the door.

"Fuck off, old man. I didn't touch your stupid dog."

"I don't believe you," I said, getting up into his face once more.

"Fuck off, or I'll fucking bash you."

I did not care. I had completely lost all sense of self control at this point. It was as if a screw had come loose somewhere. I screamed at him again, and he pushed me once more. This time I did fall, hitting the back of my head on the ground. I was momentarily dazed.

The first thing I became aware of was a thumping in my side causing ripples of pain along my ribs. I tried to turn to see what was happening. Bennett was kicking me in the side. Repeatedly. The next things that happened seemed to happen in slow motion.

Bennett took a step back with a sudden look of fear in his eyes. Chris stepped over me, his right fist swinging in a wide arc. Bennett tried to block the blow, lifting his arm. His defence was feeble, only succeeding in pushing the incoming fist upwards to connect him on the side of the head and not the chin. Bennett reeled, and was in no position to block Chris' follow up left hook. It hit him squarely on the jaw. Bennett went down like the sack of shit he was.

A pair of hands slid under my elbows and started pulling me to my feet. I glanced over my shoulder and saw it was Sada who was helping me up. I looked back to the confrontation.

Bennett was staying down. He had one arm raised in protection. I could see fear in his eyes. I won't lie. I enjoyed seeing that fear. He deserved to be afraid. He was breathing hard through his mouth, and his teeth were covered in blood. Chris stood over him. He was yelling, but I was too dazed to make sense of the words.

Sada got me to my feet and helped me slowly stagger back to the motorhome, where I vomited once more.

10

"You were supposed to keep the peace," Margaret admonished me, "not raise the bloody threat level to defcon three."

I sat at the table in the motorhome, my head resting in my hands. I did not need the lecture. I was well aware of my failings in what happened just now. But I was getting one anyway. There was no avoiding that.

"I know you love that dog," she continued, "but you can't go around picking fights based on fact-less accusations."

"He did it, Margaret," I answered in a small show of defiance. "He killed her. I know it."

"You know nothing. You have no evidence. For all we know, she's probably just run away."

"She never runs away. He did it. I'm sure of it. She's probably buried somewhere. Or he could have weighed her down and sunk her to the bottom of that damn dam."

She slid a plate of fried eggs and toast on the table in front of me. My breakfast.

"Listen to you. Damn dam. You sound like the baby of the Flintstones."

"That was Bamm-Bamm, and he was the son of the Rubbles. Now stop changing the subject."

She sat down opposite me and pulled my arms away from my face so she could look me in the eye.

"Look," she began, her voice softer now. "We haven't really mounted a proper search for her yet. Why don't you eat your breakfast and when you feel up to it, go for a walk? You can go up that hill. Take your whistle and binoculars. You'll get a better view up there. Maybe you'll spot her."

"Maybe," I conceded, though I did not have faith in the plan.

She pushed the plate under my nose.

"Good," she said, effectively stating the discussion was now over. "Now while you eat, I'm going to go outside and see what damage this latest stunt has caused."

"Maybe it's a good thing."

"What is?"

"Chris flooring Bennett."

She frowned and crossed her arms. Evidently, she did not agree. "And how could that be a good thing?"

"Well maybe now Bennett will stop acting like a bully with his rules. Maybe he'll stop pushing us around and ripping us off."

"And maybe he'll kick us all off his property. We'd be stuck with nowhere to stay in the middle of a pandemic. Had you considered that?"

She did not wait for an answer. She turned and pushed the door open. The door had slammed shut before I even had a chance to speak.

"Bennett wouldn't dare," I mumbled to myself, "he'd be too scared of Chris now to try that."

But Margaret had raised a point that did give me a moment of thought. Where were we safer? Out there, amid a deadly virus and strict lockdown, or in here with a rotten host always causing trouble? Probably in here, I decided, especially now that Bennett was tamed.

I finished my breakfast and washed up quickly. I did not feel great, and probably should be lying down and resting after the incident this morning, but I was torn with worry for Maisy. I took a couple of aspirins for the aching in my head and the throbbing from my ribs. It would have to do for now. I had a quick shower, found my binoculars and decided to set out as Margaret had suggested.

Outside, I spotted Margaret talking with Chris. She was quite diminutive next to him, but judging from his crossed arms and the set of his posture, he was on the defensive. He was probably getting a similar lecture to me. I silently wished him luck.

Matsui and Sada sat by the fire, looking downcast. I could not blame them. Spear Creek Farm was not exactly giving them the best of Australian experiences.

There was no sign of Bennett.

I did not acknowledge any of them as I passed through the camp. I was a little embarrassed about the scene I had caused earlier. That, and the fact that I had needed their rescuing.

I passed the dam and the site of the kangaroo corpse. The flies were still thick in the air and the buzzing was clearly audible from the path. I was not going to make the same mistake twice by going back there. I passed the site and walked on.

There were a lot of wild, overgrown fields in the estate, and very little in the way of red gum trees for cover. Most of the area had been cleared, and, as I walked, I could not help but be awed by the size of the place. To command such extensive space, this must have been quite a successful sheep station once upon a time. I tried imaging it in its prime, fields full of grazing sheep, their bodies artificially fattened by a layer of soft wool. It was hard to imagine what could have brought such a large, thriving sheep station so far down that not a single animal remained. What level of mismanagement could have caused it to come to this? Bennett had a lot to answer for.

At the base of the hill I found my first patch of genuine solid shade under a small grove of red gums. I sat to get some much-needed rest and to cool off. The day was already getting quite hot and it was no doubt going to be another scorcher. I took a swig from my water bottle and leaned against a tree. It was quite relaxing here, and I could quite easily sit here for hours. It was safe and quiet, with only the occasional bird call interrupting my solitude.

As I was getting to my feet, I noticed some strange markings on one tree. I brushed down my pants and walked over. It was quite an extraordinary set of markings. There were three great wedges chipped out of one tree, and similar wedges cut from another. It was as though someone with a great axe had struck them. But these could not be the mark of an axeman. The divots were too high and too large. The marks looked fresh, too, judging from the recently dried sap around the edges of the marks. It was very strange.

The hill was not too steep, but with my ribs and head still aching a little, it was far more laborious than it would have ordinarily have been for me. I was sweating and breathing hard as

I ascended the hill, and had to stop numerous times to rest. At last I reached the summit.

The view was every bit, and more, what Chris had said. To the west of the hill rose the ranges, running from the north to the south. It was beautiful mountainous land, dappled with red gums and long grass. I loved mountain views. It was something I felt we lacked more of in this wide, flat brown land of ours.

Looking back towards the farm and beyond. The fields stretched behind the farmhouse some way, before giving way to thicker bushlands. There was a thin line of water, as Chris had said, which must have been Spear Creek. It was all very rural and pretty. I wish I had remembered to bring my camera.

I retrieved my binoculars from their case and levelled them on the camp. Margaret sat under the annex of the motorhome, deeply engaged in a book. She had a pencil in her hand, and I assumed she was working through one of her sudoku puzzles. She would randomly swat at the air. A persistent fly must have been bothering her.

I moved the binoculars over to Sada and Matsui. Sada had coaxed her up from her hangover doldrums and was trying to get a game of frisbee going with her. Her energy levels were low, and she walked slowly each time to pick up the thrown frisbee. Her clothes were skimpy and revealing. Her top was merely a thin fabric that covered her chest from just below the armpit to just under the ribcage, exposing her flat stomach and highlighting her small breasts. Her tan shorts were small and tight, doing as much to 'cover her' as the top. My binoculars lingered on Matsui a few moments, but I soon moved them away out of guilt. I was fifty-seven years old. I should not be looking at young girls like that. I was not a pervert.

I moved my glasses to the farmhouse. I could see Bennett through the glass door. He appeared to be watching Sada and Matsui as they went about their game. He had one hand down his pants. I looked away. Just the very sight of him made me sick, and the idea of him fondling himself while watching Matsui only made me hate him more.

I looked for Chris next. He was far beyond the farmhouse, walking through the thicker bushland beyond the fields. Under the crook of one arm he held numerous thick, long sticks. Fuel for the coming night's fire.

Next, I scanned the length of the boundaries of the property. The boundary fence looked mostly new, providing a stark contrast to the fences that circled the inner paddocks, which hung loosely from their posts and bore signs of rust in comparison. I found it odd that this had been updated and fixed when so much else sat in such a state of disrepair. Was there really a great need for the upkeep on them? There was also hoops of barbed wire around the top of the fence that surrounded the property. It seemed needlessly wasteful. I highly doubted Bennett needed such heavy security to keep people out. What was there to steal? There were no sheep left.

There was no sign of Maisy that I could see, so I turned my binoculars to the ranges. The ranges were beautiful. At one point I saw a large bird soaring majestically over the mountains. I thought it may have been a wedge-tailed eagle, but I could not be sure. There were many shadows and crevices in the mountains, and it took time to scan across them. After an hour under the high, baking sun, I finally gave up.

There was no sign of Maisy anywhere.

11

When I arrived back at the camp, the sun was high and hot. Chris had collected a large pile of wood by the fire. More, perhaps, than what was needed, but maybe he was getting a head start on tomorrow's collection. Nobody was around, and Bennett could no longer be seen through the glass sliding door, so I headed for the motorhome.

Everyone (excluding the vile Bennett of course) had gathered inside to enjoy the air-conditioned comfort and to escape the burning heat. Matsui was still in her skimpy outfit, which seemed even more gratuitous up close. Chris looked calm and relaxed.

"Any luck, dear?" Margaret asked as I entered.

I shook my head sadly. "Not a single sign of her anywhere."

I opened the refrigerator to get a fresh water and soon joined the group. They had been discussing food and Australian wildlife. More specifically, which Australian wildlife could be eaten. It seemed Sada had been on quite the culinary tour since arriving and eaten a fair range of our local fauna.

"I've tried emu, crocodile, kangaroo and lots of fish like barramundi," he boasted proudly.

"What about yabbies? Have you tried yabbies yet?" Chris asked.

"What is a yabby?"

"You've never heard of a yabby? You're missing out, Sada. They're like a freshwater lobster, but they're about the size of a prawn. You boil them up in hot water and eat the meat from their tails."

"Ah. Where can I buy these yabbies?"

"You can get them at the seafood markets just like any fish." Suddenly a light went on in Chris' eyes and he raised a finger. "You know what, I reckon there'd be yabbies in the dam. We should go yabbying. Does anybody have any fresh meat?"

Margaret's face dropped and I could swear I saw her shrink at least a foot. "Chris," she said in a voice I'd heard many times over in the past any time I had suggested we do something ludicrously stupid, "I really don't think that's a good idea. You've seen how Bennett reacts every time we break one of his rules. You saw how he was yesterday when you were just skimming rocks. I think you should stay away from his dam."

"Bennett," Chris snorted, "don't worry about him. He won't bother us unless he wants another fat lip."

"Chris, I really can't condone more violence."

"It won't come to that. Bennett just needed sorting out. And I've done that now. His rules are silly. Besides, what harm is there in a little bit of yabbying in his dam?"

Margaret looked at me with beseeching eyes. If I knew my place in this world, it was beside her and supporting her views.

"She's right, Chris," I added, "we should probably stick to the rules and keep the peace a bit. At least for a day."

"Bah" said Chris, "I'm not falling under the heel of dictator Bennett. What's he going to do? Not get my shopping for me? I don't care. I'll go hungry for a few days and then get out of here. Or maybe I'll eat fresh yabbies in that time. Who cares? I'd rather that than doing only the things Bennett says I can do."

I didn't think we were going to get through to him.

"I want to try yabbies," Sada added unhelpfully.

Margaret rolled her eyes and stood up to walk away from the table. "I'm not having any part of that. You'll have to find your own meat."

"We have meat," Matsui joined the fray. The tide was definitely against us now.

"Excellent," chimed up Chris, "do you have any fishing wire or string?"

I had both, but the hard stare from Margaret told me I had better keep it to myself.

"I think so, we'll go and look," said Sada.

I got out of the way to make room for everybody to get up and go outside. Before long it was just Margaret and I alone in the motorhome once more. She let out a long sigh.

"I can't stand this," she said, "every second minute it feels like we're headed for more conflict. I can't even bear to watch." She looked at me and I shrugged. They were adults. It was not up to me to make the decisions for everyone and I doubted they would listen if I tried to. I was much politer than Bennett, but they still had free wills of their own.

"You'd better go too," Margaret said at last, "just to keep an eye on them. But promise me this time you'll try and keep the peace, not start wars."

"You got it, Hot Lips."

I went to kiss her, but she did not turn her lips to mine. Still angry. I pecked her on the cheek before stepping outside.

I could see Chris, Sada and Matsui all huddled near their tent. Chris was tying a cube of meat to the end of a long string. I glanced over to the farmhouse. No sign of Bennett in the windows that I could see, but that did not mean he was not watching. Then I glanced at the shed with the bullet holes. He could easily seclude himself there, too, and watch. It would be bloody hot though.

I walked over to the group, who did not look up as I approached.

"You joining us, Paul?" Chris asked as he pulled his knot tight on the string.

"Yeah, I've come to watch," I said.

"Great," Chris said without emotion. He finished his work and held it up, bouncing on the meat on the string to ensure it held. He then made second line while Matsui filled a pot with water for the catch and Sada found a couple of sticks.

Chris quickly tied the non-meat end of the string to the sticks with a basic double knot and set off towards the dam. I followed slowly behand, regularly glancing over my shoulder towards the farmhouse. I expected at any moment for Bennett to come out ranting and raving. But there was no movement from the house.

We arrived at the dam's edge and Chris threw the meat out into the muddy water. He then stabbed the sticks into the ground and sat to wait. I glanced once more at the farmhouse. Nothing. Perhaps Chris was right. Perhaps the balance of power had changed. As long as Bennett was subdued, we may finally have some freedoms and order here on Spear Creek Farm.

Chris, Sada and Matsui all seemed to be quite relaxed as we sat by the dam, chatting and laughing as we waited for the strings to go taut. I could not relax, and found myself regularly checking over my shoulder. I sensed Bennett's hateful gaze on my back. It was probably just my imagination, but it was a feeling I just could not shake.

Suddenly Matsui jumped up and squealed. I jumped, thinking something had gone wrong when I realised it was a squeal of excitement. One of the lines had gone taut.

"Right," said Chris, "take the line and bring it in slowly. Then, once you see it on the edge, pull it quickly ashore. I'll grab the first one to show you how it's done."

Matsui did as Chris had instructed. There was a palpable sense of excitement from her and Sada. They stared intensely at the water as they pulled the line in and almost jumped at the first sight of the yabby. Matsui yanked the line, pulling the yabby onto the bank. Chris leapt into action, grabbing the yabby by the back between his thumb and forefinger.

The yabby looked very much like a miniature lobster, right down to the claws, legs and tail. Yabbies, however, were brown in colour, helping them camouflage themselves for hunting but also hide from their own predators in the muddy water of the dam. It was a big one, almost as big as Chris' hand. The claws of the yabby opened and closed as it snapped at the air in a useless attempt to fight off its oppressor. Despite its size, it could still give you a painful nip if you let it.

"It's ugly," Matsui giggled.

"No way, this is a beauty," Chris said. "A few more big ones like this and we'll have tonight's dinner sorted."

He checked under the tail to ensure there was no eggs there before dropping the yabby into the pot.

I glanced over my shoulder towards the house once more. Still nothing from Bennett. Perhaps Chris was right and he had been subdued after all.

The yabbying progressed and I found myself starting to relax. Chris began telling stories about his own camping experiences with his father, including a tall tale of a yabbying haul the two of them produced in one afternoon that was too fantastical to be believed.

Two more yabbies soon filled the pot and our conversation levels rose and rose with the exaggeration of Chris' stories and our own laughter.

Then came the gunshot.

A plume of dust kicked up near us and rocks spat outwards from the point of impact. For a moment I was stunned. My mind could not register what had happened. Then there was a second shot.

I jumped to my feet and turned. I did not know why I did this. I was only making myself an easier target, but my mind was a blur and still coming to terms with what was happening.

"Get down, you idiot" Chris hissed.

I saw Bennett coming from the house towards us. He was looking at us through the sights of the hunting rifle that nestled into his shoulder. He was red faced and sweaty, and his eyes were wide.

"Get up," he screamed. "Get up now."

There was an edge to his voice. A hysteria. There had always been a rudeness and aggressiveness in his manner towards us, but this seemed a little more... panicked? I could not put my finger on it.

I raised my hands as the others nervously rose to their feet around me. I cast a glance at Chris. He looked like he had just bitten into a lemon. A very sour one.

"You fucking people," Bennett yelled as he got closer. "You're forgetting where you are. This is *my* land, and on *my* land, you follow *my* rules."

I stepped back as he came close. His face was screwed up in rage, and I could see the fat lip where Chris had hit him. He pointed his gun at each of us in turn. Chris, Sada and Matsui all raised their hands. He came closer. I thought for a moment he was about to poke me in the chest with the gun.

"Are you scared, old man?" he sneered. "Well you should be. You all need to remember this is my property and while you are all here in this lockdown, I am in command. Do you understand? In this lockdown, on my property, I am the law."

To make his point, he lowered the weapon a moment and kicked over the pot of yabbies. Now on the ground, they kicked their tails and flipped towards the water.

Chris' eyes were burning with hatred. I could see from the corners of my eyes he was slowly clenching and unclenching his fists. I slowly gulped, praying Chris would maintain self-control. There was no telling what might happen.

The air hung thick with tension. A fly buzzed past my ear and started circling my face. It landed on my nose, and then started walking up my nose towards my eye. I desperately wanted to swat at it, but I did not dare to move. I blinked rapidly as it closed on my eye. I must have brushed it with my eyelash, and it flew away. I let out the breath I had been holding.

When Bennett had moved to kick the pot, Chris and Sada moved one way, and Matsui the other. I noticed that Matsui was now separated from the three of us on the opposite side of Bennett. Or, to put it a better way, isolated. Bennett noticed it too.

He took one step back and looked at her. His slimy eyes looked her up and down, lingering far too long on her breasts. A greasy smile came over his features.

"You've given me headaches since you've arrived. All of you. Maybe I need to teach you a lesson. Remind you who's in charge here so there won't be any more incidents like this morning. No more misunderstandings."

He turned to Matsui once more, his depraved eyes sliding down her form once more.

"You," he said, "show me your tits."

The words were blunt and they hit like a hammer. Matsui suddenly looked fearful and Sada went red with anger. If the incident from this morning took us to defcon three, we had just moved to defcon one. If he forced this, there was no turning back.

"Bennett I'm not sure…" I stuttered.

Bennett swung his gun on me and stuck it right up close in my face. The barrel was a mere inch from my eyes.

"Shut up," he screamed, "just shut up. Or I will kill you now. Kill all of you."

In that moment, I believed him. He paused a moment, his finger resting on the trigger, looking down the sights at me. I saw nothing behind that eye. No remorse. No feeling. No humanity.

Slowly he pulled back and half turned back towards Matsui.

"Right," he continued, "I hope it should be clear to you all now I'm not fucking around. My place, my rules. I'm instituting Marshall Law. I'll shoot the next person who breaks one of my rules. You obey curfew. You stay away from my dam. Understood?"

Nobody moved or said anything.

"Understood?" he shouted.

I nodded. The others did too.

"Right. Good. We're finally getting some fucking order around here. Now, show me those tits."

My legs started turning to jelly and I felt sick. Sick for Matsui. Up until then I had thought demand had just been a way for him to flex his muscles. Show us who was boss. Show us that if he wanted to, he could get us to do anything. I thought it just a hollow threat. But the demand had come back, and in the back of my mind I recalled that drawer full of pornography. His Asian fetish.

"We'll obey from now on," Chris said, "we'll do everything you say. But please. There's no need to humiliate her."

"Shut up," Bennett growled, and for a second I thought he would step forward and put the gun in Chris' face too. But he held back. Maybe he held a small inkling of fear of Chris after the beating this morning. Enough to make him hold back. He stared at Chris a bit longer, and then turned to Matsui.

"Now. Pull down your top. Show me those tits."

Matsui was crying now. She shook her head, squeezing her eyes shut as tears rolled down her cheeks.

I gritted my teeth. I had never before in my life felt the urge to kill someone. I had enemies through life. I had bosses that treated me like absolute crap. I had been teased and beaten up in school by bullies. They had all genuinely treated me like garbage, and I hated them for it. But I never wanted to kill a man. Not until Bennett in this moment. Killing him would be a mercy. The world would be a better place for it.

From the looks on Chris and Sada's faces, I expected they felt much the same. I wished there was some way we could have communicated. Maybe if we all jumped him, at once, we could put an end to it. He could not take all three of us. One of us might have to take a bullet though. Who? Logically, I would be the better choice. I was old. I had lived a full life. They were young. They had so much to live for. So much they could still do for the world.

Perhaps if I leapt at Bennett now, I could take a bullet and then they could take him down. This time they could tie him up. Get the police. Get an ambulance for me. Maybe there would be time to save me. Maybe not.

But no. I could not do it. I could not risk my life like that. I still had much to live for. I had a grandchild coming. I needed to make sure Margaret got there for the birth. In fact, getting Margaret to Perth in time was the one thing in the world I cared about most. I would sit out in the motorhome if Jane made me, but there is no way I could let Margaret miss it. Not this. Not when it meant so much to her.

And Jane. Could I really leave this mortal coil before we'd had the chance to reconcile? Could I really do something stupid, like jump at Bennett now and take the shot, just so the others could stop him? No, I could not do that to Jane. I could not let her live the rest of her life with the guilt of not having forgiven her father before he died.

This was no time for heroics. Not now.

"Do it," Bennett yelled once more. "Get those fucking tits out."

Matsui continued to shake her head. Bennett grunted and started blowing hard from his nose. He was getting frustrated. He stepped sideways closer to her. He adjusted his grip on the gun, keeping it trained on Chris, who stood in the middle of Sada and I. With one hard still holding the rifle awkwardly, his finger still hovering over the trigger, he reached out with the other to grab Matsui's top and attempted to pull it down. Matsui's hands came down immediately to clutch at her chest. Chris and Sada stepped forward and Bennett abandoned his attempt to pull down Matsui's top to fix his grip and train the gun on them. They froze. Matsui fell to the ground sobbing.

Bennett stared at them for a moment, then laughed. It came across as false and hollow. Attempted bravado. I was not buying it. He saw it now. He knew if we all jumped him at once he would not stand a chance.

"Alright. I think we have an understanding now. You obey my rules. You do what I say. Or you become yabby food. Got it?" He glanced down at Matsui and smirked. "I'll leave your little slut alone. For now."

She looked up sharply at that last remark. He blew her a kiss and started backing away with the gun still trained on us. Slowly he made his way back to his house. We all stood motionless, watching. I held my breath. He reached the house and slipped through the sliding door. I breathed out at last, though it did not relieve the tension I felt.

Sada went to console Matsui. She pushed him away. There was a quick exchange in Japanese. He was pleading, but she wanted nothing to do with him. She got to her feet, still crying and pushing him away. He would not let her be, standing in front of her and talking as she tried walking off.

"Let her go," Margaret said. I turned. I was not aware she had come from the motorhome but she must have witnessed everything. "She needs space. Let her go alone. She will come back to you when she needs you."

Sada paused, and looked at Margaret. After a moment he nodded, and bowed his head. Matsui walked away.

Chris had not moved since Bennett went into the house. He stood like a statue. Staring.

"I'm going to kill that son of a bitch," he said, his tone dark and murderous.

I tried to lighten the mood. "Ah, you know Bennett. It's like you say, Chris, Premier League dickhead."

His stony eyes swivelled to me. "I'm past jokes with this guy, Paul. He threatened us with a gun. He tried to humiliated Matsui. This shit has got to stop."

"Nobody's killing anyone," Margaret said, her voice a motherly command. "We need to contact the police. They need to come here and deal with it, not us."

"And how are you going to do that, Margaret?" Chris asked. "There's no mobile signal here. I've walked everywhere on the property. I couldn't get a single bar on my phone, and I'm on the best network in Australia."

"Bennett has a phone," Sada added.

"I don't think Bennett will let us borrow it," I snorted, but quickly went silent. Another failed attempt to lighten the situation.

"No, he won't," Chris agreed. He turned to look at the farmhouse once more. "We'll have to take it ourselves."

"No," Margaret said, "this can't continue. We need to cool down. No more hot-headed decisions. There must be a way to get in touch with the outside world. We just need to think it through. There's a way. We just need to come up with it."

I nodded.

Sada and Chris did too. But I think they only did it to appease Margaret. Their eyes were still set on the farmhouse. They were thinking something else entirely.

12

Margaret and I sat alone in the air-conditioned comfort of our motorhome. Sada and Chris had decided not to join us, opting instead to stay out in the baking sun. Matsui had yet to return, and they wanted to keep an eye on the house to make sure Bennett remained there.

At regular intervals, Margaret made me get up and glance through the window to check on them. She was worried they might attempt some form of retribution. But they remained seated. Watching the house like hawks.

"Are they talking to each other?" she asked.

"Yes, I think so."

"Probably scheming on how to take Bennett. Paul, we need to work out a way out of this. I don't trust them to. They both had murder in their eyes when Bennett had the gun on them. Anything they come up with will only lead to more violence."

I resumed my seat opposite her and took her hands.

"I was thinking about that. Maybe we should just pack the van and leave. What's actually keeping us here? A lockdown? We should just get out onto the road and drive until we find a policeman or we get a signal and report Bennett. They surely wouldn't force us back after this. It's not safe. They might put us into quarantine or something, but once they hear about Bennett, I doubt they'll force us back."

She stared at me for a moment then her face broke into a smile.

"Of course," she said, "it's so obvious. I can't believe it was staring me in the face all along. I was so caught up in the lockdown I forgot the only thing keeping us here was us."

I frowned. My lip quivered a little.

"Yes, us. But also, Maisy."

"Oh," she frowned. She looked deep into my eyes and I broke contact to look down. "You don't want to leave though, do you? You think Maisy will come back?"

"I do, yes. But maybe we can come back after, and find her then?"

"Why don't we suggest the plan to the others? It might be better if Sada and Matsui left anyway. Especially after today."

"Ok, I'll go out there and talk to Chris and Sada. We'll work something out. You stay here out of the heat."

I gave Margaret a quick peck on the cheek before exiting the motorhome. The mid-afternoon sun was baking hot and I had no idea how Chris and Sada could sit openly under it. I could see Chris' neck reddening with sunburn. I pointed it out but he did not seem to care. They were both focused on watching Bennett, so I decided to get quickly to the point.

"Margaret and I were talking. We think someone needs to leave here. Go and get the police and bring them back here."

Chris looked up. He considered me for a moment, before standing up and brushing his clothes down. "Come," he said, "I want to show you something."

He walked towards the house. I followed, not sure what I was getting involved in now. I thought for a while we were heading to another confrontation when Chris abruptly turned and began walking up the driveway. The gravel cracked as it moved underfoot, and I tried to look into the house's windows as we passed. The curtains were shut tight but I knew he was in there. I doubted he could get past the watchdog stares of Sada and Chris.

The head of the driveway was marked by the big gate we passed through yesterday. Chris gestured towards it. I was again struck by the heaviness of it. It had a solid, thick steel frame. The gate was closed.

"Did you look at this closely when you came in?" Chris said.

"Not in great detail, why?"

"Have a look at it again. It's electric. It won't open without the control. Try shifting it."

I looked at it again. There was a large electrical box on one side connected with a series of thick gears. I approached the gate and gave it a solid pull. I could not even shift it an inch. I gave it a few seconds of effort before pulling away from it, puffing.

I could see the road beyond the gate. Only a few tree lined meters away. The road was completely devoid of traffic, much like the day we arrived.

"OK, he probably won't give us the control," I concluded. "Maybe we could lift your motorbike over?"

"And then what? Drop it on the other side?"

He was right. I was not thinking straight.

"How far are we from the next farm, or any other place?"

"I don't know. Far. You're not thinking of climbing over the fence and walking, are you?"

I had considered it. Maybe not me, but one of us. I did not like the feeling of isolation here at Spear Creek Farm. I was starting to feel trapped. And not because of lockdown. It really felt like Bennett had imprisoned us.

Suddenly a shot rang out.

We both jumped, turning quickly. Bennett stood halfway down the driveway. His rifle pointed into the air. Ten meters behind him stood Sada. He glanced back at Sada and then pointed the gun at us. Counting the incident from earlier in the day, this was the second time in my life I had had a gun pointed at me. I did not like that this was becoming a habit.

"Get away from there," Bennett yelled to us. "I'm making the gate another prohibited area. Nobody is allowed near it. So, move the fuck on. Now."

I glanced at Chris, who nodded for me to move away. I started walking back down the driveway. I was starting to feel even more like a prisoner with each passing moment. No matter what we did, the situation only got worse.

13

The mood around the camp remained sombre for the best part of the day.

Matsui returned, though she showed little interest in engaging with anyone. Sada was extra attentive, though his efforts only worsened the situation, and soon they had stopped talking with each other altogether. Matsui sat quietly and alone while Sada focused his fiery glare at the farmhouse.

Chris had changed too. Margaret suggested privately to me that his pride had taken a blow after his alpha male status was stripped. That may have been part of it. The other part may have been that feeling when standing on the wrong end of a gun held by Bennett. I had felt it too. It was sobering. And scary.

When I told Margaret about the gate, she became quite introspective and I could see the lines on her brow furrow with worry. She was always concerned with the escalating tensions in the camp. Now, it seemed, it had gone beyond repair. The only question was, what would happen next?

Thankfully, though, the day rolled on without further incident.

Bennett, as he had the day prior, stayed in his house with the curtains drawn tight and kept to himself. I wondered what he did in there. I had only seen one half of the house when I snooped around, surely there was something else to it? Was he playing video games? Working an online job? The only thing I could conclude with any certainty was this: he was not cleaning.

We invited Chris, Sada and Matsui into our air-conditioned motorhome when the afternoon heat was hitting its peak. They welcomed the invitation, but as we sat around the table it was like attending a wake. I could not stand it. I went out to search for Maisy. It was too hot to be walking about and climbing hills, especially at my age, but I preferred that over staying inside the suffocating gloom of the motorhome.

As I stood atop the hill, I scanned the surrounding fences again. The glinting barbed wire and solid frames took on a more sinister look to them today, as if my change in mood had altered the light in which I viewed them. Perhaps it was the incident at the gate. The way he forced us away at gunpoint. I was not sure. But as I looked at the boundary fence now, I could not help but think they were designed to keep people in, not keep them out.

I had to stop looking. My thoughts were running away from me and becoming far too macabre. Surely just flights of fancy from an imagination affected by a negative experience? I hoped so.

There was still no sign of Maisy. I blew on the whistle several times and scanned the farm and surrounds over and over with no success. Maisy was gone.

I trudged back into camp and back into our motorhome. The wake was still in progress. After I had rested and cooled down, I noticed a crust of salt on my brow and over my body. When the heat of the day finally passed, Margaret ended the wake to allow me to clean off in a shower. As I came out, Margaret was waiting for me.

"How are things with the gang?" I asked.

She sighed. "Not good. Sada is very angry, but Chris has gone into his shell. I don't think there will be any further incidents today. Thank God. Not unless Bennett starts something."

I agreed. But that was the worry. What if Bennett did start something? What then?

As had become the norm, we all met by the fire later that night. It was my turn to choose the wine and I went with a Shiraz we had picked up from the Adelaide Hills. It was a good wine, but I had no taste for drinking.

Chris retired early. I tried to get Sada and Matsui talking again when Margaret pinched me. I was not saying anything wrong, but I knew why. It was time to give them space. Time to leave them alone and hope they could open up to each other and begin the healing process. We left with half of the Shiraz undrunk.

Despite all the concerns and worries that raged through my mind, I dropped quickly into sleep. Perhaps the long walk in the afternoon had taken it out of me, and with a drop of red to cap things off, I doubted I could have stayed awake if I had tried.

Margaret and I woke at the same time and we decided that this morning it would be just the two of us. We were not going to open the door, let the others and their moods come in and ruin our breakfast. We were going to have a happy breakfast with positive thoughts and enjoy each other's company. It was our way of conquering the gloom of yesterday and starting this day positively.

We could not stay in our home all day though. I wanted to go in search of Maisy. I was not giving up on her. After eating and cleaning, I left Margaret to her sudoku book and went outside to go for a walk.

Chris sat slumped in a fold up chair in front of the firepit. He had a jumble of twigs and grass in his lap and was throwing each scrap one by one into the glowing coals. A thin line of smoke emerged from the fire, which glared malevolently red. There was no sign of Sada or Matsui, and their tent was zipped shut.

I greeted Chris and asked after Sada and Matsui. I was hoping they had grabbed hold of the opportunity we gave them last night and healed that rift. He had not seen them yet and assumed they were still sleeping. I looked at my watch. It was almost eleven and it was already quite hot. It was hard to imagine they were still asleep.

I walked past the dam and along the track just like yesterday. I climbed the hill a third time in two days and had the same success level in my quest as I did the first two times. Maisy was gone. I needed to start accepting it. Either she had run off or Bennett had done something to her. There was no way to prove either was true. It did not matter anyway. It was time I had to let go.

I spent less time scanning the farm and hills for traces of Maisy and more time scanning the roads this time. I must have watched for over an hour without sighting a single vehicle. I had started thinking that even if we were unable to get out, maybe there was some way of flagging a passing vehicle to come to us. We could signal the driver to pull over and talk. We could report Bennett. Report him pointing a gun on us. His attempted assault on Matsui.

But no cars came down the road.

When the day's heat became too much to bear, I moved on. I descended the hill and walked back to camp, pondering what other moves we might have.

Sada and Matsui had still not emerged from their tent when I returned. Chris had not moved and his skin was reddening under the sun.

"You'd better put some sun screen on mate, you're already starting to burn."

Chris jumped. I had not intended to sneak up but he was so deeply lost in his thoughts that he failed to notice me. He smiled and reached for his neck. It already looked angry and red, and judging from how quickly he jumped to put sunscreen on, it must have felt burning hot too.

"Did you see Sada and Matsui on your walk?" Chris asked as he started squeezing the cream from the tube.

"No, I didn't. How were they this morning? Are they talking now?"

Chris stopped and looked at me strangely. "Like I said before, I haven't seen them. I was just assuming we were wrong before. That maybe they got up and went for a walk before I got up. They can't still be asleep in there. Not in this heat."

Chris dropped the sunscreen bottle and looked me in the eye. Something clicked. It clicked in me too. We turned to their tent and approached it.

"Sada. Matsui. Are you in there, guys?"

There was no answer. We walked up to the tent and tried calling again. Still nothing. We crouched down in front of the front entrance. Chris reached out to the zipper, clasping it between his fingers. He looked at me with a question in his eyes. I nodded my approval. He unzipped the tent.

The tent was empty. Completely and utterly empty. No bedding. No mattress. Nothing.

Chris took a slow, deep breath and then closed the zip once more. He stood up, stepped away and sat by the dying dire once more. I remained crouched a moment, trying to reconcile what I saw. What had I expected? Sada and Matsui still asleep? Untidy bedding? No, I had not expected anything. But I had definitely not expected nothing. And nothing was far more chilling than anything I could have imagined.

I stood up and walked to their car. I looked through the windows and into the hatchback. I expected to see all the bedding, sleeping bags, whatever in there. Packed up and ready to go. There was nothing in there either.

"Get away from there," Chris said, his voice dead and monotone, "before Bennett sees you snooping."

"Bennett? Why would he care if I'm looking at their stuff?"

Chris' eyes swivelled to meet mine. They were devoid of anything. Emotion. Feeling. Life.

"Don't you get it, Paul? He's killed them. Bennett has killed Sada and Matsui."

I looked up at the house. The curtains moved as someone ducked behind them. It was too late. Bennett had already been watching us.

14

We had to stand in Margaret's way to stop her from going and seeing for herself. I stood by the door leading outside the motorhome, and Chris by the table.

She did not believe us. To be honest, I could barely believe what I was saying myself. But since Chris had said it, I had no doubts. Sada and Matsui were dead. Bennett had murdered them. There was no other explanation.

"But how can you be so sure?" Margaret asked.

"They are gone, and so is everything from their tent," Chris stated. "Their car is untouched. Their tent is still up. They would not just go out for a walk with everything they had inside their tent."

"But why would Bennett take everything out of their tents?"

"Maybe they had blood on them," I said.

They both looked at me, and I immediately regretted saying it. The words had just spilled out. Just like they always did.

Margaret's eyes widened and I think she started to believe. She slumped back into the seat, taking the news in. I myself had only just began to reconcile it in my own mind. Accept that it had happened. And I had only one thing on my mind now. We needed escape.

As we talked, I realised Chris was in the same place as me. He was a changed man. He no longer sought out confronting Bennett. He wanted to actively avoid him. Chris had definitely changed. He was scared.

Margaret, once she had accepted Sada and Matsui's disappearance as suspicious, soon joined the headspace Chris and I were already in. Bennett was dangerous and unpredictable. It was not safe for us in Spear Creek Farm any more. We needed to get out of here, and we needed to do it soon. If Bennett had seen us investigating the tent and car, who knew how long it would be before he came for us next?

That is when we started formulating our escape plan.

We talked about the gate first. That was our biggest obstacle. There was no way we were getting this big motorhome out any other way than through that gate, and we were not going anywhere without the motorhome. Could you imagine the three of us huddled on the back of Chris' bike? I couldn't.

Margaret suggested we should just help Chris escape on his motorbike and return with the authorities. But Chris would have nothing of it. He made us make a pact. All of us were getting out, together. I made a joke that it should be a blood pact. Yet another comment I wished I could take back.

We considered ramming the gate. It was thick, we might get through, but the damage to the motorhome would be considerable. What if the motorhome would not run after that? We would be stuck with just Chris' motorbike, and we had already written off the plan around all of us together on that. The noise would pretty quickly summon Bennett too. No. Smashing our way out was too risky. We could do it, but only as a last resort. We needed to try something else first.

Next, we considered creeping through the fence in the night and walking. The fence, as far as I saw, was topped by barbed wire the whole way around. There was no way over it, but if we had some clippers, which I'm sure I had somewhere, we could make a hole and escape. But then there was Margaret's knee. She would not be able to handle a lengthy walk. And how far would we even need to walk? There had not been a car going past the property that we had seen in days, and there was no knowing how long we would walk for.

No, we needed the motorhome. And so, we came back to the problem of the gate.

We worked all through the afternoon on it. We threw ideas and scenarios at each other. We weighed up each other's ideas. We developed lists. We went over every option we could think of. There was not a single plan that did not involve an element of risk. The risk, of course, being Bennett catching us in the act. And what happened then? We could not say.

We finally came up with a plan close to dinner. It was not perfect. Not by any stretch of the imagination. But it was the best we could do, and we were doing it tonight. Before Bennett had the chance to strike again.

We cooked a quick pasta. It was just sauce from a jar and cooked spaghetti. We were too distracted to put a proper meal together. It did not matter. I could not eat anyhow. I was too nervous. I tried a few mouthfuls but I felt queasy and pushed my plate aside. I would not eat until we were a long way from here.

After eating, Chris left our motorhome to start the fire for the evening. We needed to ensure that it looked like any other night. We did not want Bennett getting suspicious or watching us too closely.

Dusk came quickly. Sada and Matsui had not appeared. Nor did we expect them to. We were more than convinced of their fates now.

The sickness that started in my stomach seemed to spread to the rest of my extremities. I could not hold my hands steady and my legs felt wobbly. Margaret and I moved about the motorhome, packing everything up and ensuring it was well stowed. As we finished, I felt her hand on my shoulder. I turned and she slid her arms around me and we hugged. It was a warm, assuring hug. It felt good.

"Just promise me," Margaret said, "no stupid risks tonight. I need you alive to take me to Perth."

"I promise. And you promise me too. I need someone to tell me how beautiful our grandchild is and how good of a mother Jane is."

Margaret pulled back from me and looked me in the eyes. "Jane will forgive you. She will. You're her father. She's angry. Zheng is angry. But they will get over it. They will. You will see."

She squeezed my arms tight as she spoke. I felt tears welling in my eyes. I wanted to believe her. I wished it was true.

We hugged again. I did not want it to stop. I did not want it to stop because I did not want to let go of Margaret, and because I did not want to face what was next.

Margaret let go first. She pulled away, and blew me a kiss. She opened the door and stepped out of the motorhome. I walked to the window and watched her walk down to the fire and join Chris at the fireside.

I stepped away from the window and took a deep breath. My stomach still felt queasy and my legs were unsteady.

One by one I started turning off all the systems in the motorhome. The air-conditioning. The lights. The refrigerator. Everything. It was dark and quiet inside. It would have made a good place to hide and hope for everything to just blow over.

I stepped outside the motorhome with a bag of rubbish. It was dark outside, and with the lights of the motorhome all off, I doubted Bennett would see me from the farmhouse. Carefully, I unclipped the poles from the annex and let it roll back inside the motorhome roof. I stowed the poles, kicked the chocks from under the wheels and walked to the other side of the motorhome. I kicked out the chocks on this side too, then approached the power and water connections. I bent down beside them, pretending to tie my shoelace. I reached out with one hand and turned the tap that connected the motorhome to the water tanks to the closed position. Finally, I reached out and unclipped the power and water cables. We were no longer connected to the farm.

I picked up the bag of rubbish and started walking towards the house. The rubbish bins were kept next to the carport. I walked directly towards the house, the aim being to glance in the windows and to get bearings on Bennett. We needed to know where he was before we tried breaking into his car.

There was one light on in the house. It was from the bedroom. The curtains were drawn, but I knew this was the bedroom from my earlier exploration of the house. I approached the house slowly, trying to find an angle from which to see inside. My heart was thumping harder and harder as I got closer and closer to the house. I walked right up to the window. There was a small crack between the curtains. I stepped forward to place my ear against the glass.

"Are you alright there, Paul?"

I jumped out of my skin. I turned to my right to see Bennett standing there. His voice was cold and his face hostile. He must have been standing in the shadows of the water tanks watching me. How long had he been watching?

I held up the plastic bag I held. "I was just dropping some trash off."

"I see that, Paul. What I don't see is a reason for you to be peeking through my windows. Are you some sort of a pervert, Paul?"

We had not prepared for this. We had not expected this. If we had, I would have a rehearsed answer ready. But I did not.

"I...I was just taking out the trash..."

"You said that already, Paul."

"... and I wanted to see if you were in and see if you wanted to join us for a drink."

Shit. Why did I say that?

Bennett raised an eyebrow. "Drink?"

"Yeah, drink."

A sardonic smile crossed his lips. "Drink with you? Why the fuck would I want to do that?" He stepped closer, and we were almost standing face to face. His rank breath blew in my face, and I did my best not cringe. "No Paul, I do not want a fucking drink with you. Now put your rubbish in the bin and fuck off to your friends by the fire."

He pushed past me, forcing me against the brickwork on the corner of the window as he passed. It pressed hard into my back and I had to stop myself from wincing. He walked to the sliding door entrance and stopped, turning back to me once more.

"Oh, and Paul, unless you want to be yabby food tonight, stay the fuck away from my house."

He went through the door and slammed it behind him. My whole body was tingling with nerves and I had to steady myself against the wall. After I few moments, I straightened and walked on. I glanced at the dam as I walked. Yabby food. That was the second time Bennett had used that threat. I started to wonder if that was what had happened to Sada and Matsui.

Another light went on in the house. Again, the view inside was obscured by curtains. It was in one of the rooms I had not explored, but judging by the shape and pattern of the window and curtains, I guessed it was probably the kitchen. I walked past the windows and house to the bins and dropped my rubbish inside. I crept back to the house and then I signalled to Chris. We had passed phase one of the plan, if only just. I had scouted the house and I knew where Bennett was. He was inside. Now for phase two. Breaking into Bennett's car.

I stood by the house and watched the lit window. Chris ran up to me in a crouched run, while Margaret set up pillows in the chairs around the fire. The silhouettes of the pillows against the firelight, if set up right, should give the impression that we all were sitting there. At least that's what we hoped.

Chris came beside me and pressed himself against the wall. "All good?" he whispered.

"Bennett caught me looking inside but I think I got away with it."

"We saw. He was doing something by the dam and then went around the back of the house. I assumed he had gone in the back door." Chris craned his neck forward to look along the length of the house. "Where is he now?"

I nodded towards the lit-up window. "Inside."

Chris pulled a string and our door stop from his pockets. At the end of the string was a small noose. Bennett's car was old, and the door lock mechanism was one of the varieties that sat on the top of the inner door panel, the type you pushed down to lock and pulled up to unlock. Chris' plan was to try and wedge the door open a little with our triangular doorstop and drop his noose over the lock, tighten it, then unlock the car by pulling the string up.

It was simple, he had said. I asked him if he had ever done it before. He gave me a knowing smile. Whoever said there was such a thing as a misspent youth?

Chris went to the car and started pulling at the top of the door, trying to create a gap between the frame and door to wedge the doorstop in. He only needed it to open a little. Enough for him to drop the string through.

I focused my attention to the window. I could tell little of what Bennett was up to. The light was still on, but if Bennett was still there, I could not say. I crept along the wall and under the window to the sliding door. There was no way to watch the back door, so hopefully if Bennett came out, he would come through here. I peered into the entrance hall. The gun hung above the counter. I stared at it a moment. I had no idea how to work a gun, but getting the gun away from Bennett may be half the battle. It would be going off script, but what good was the plan if it did not allow for new opportunities as they presented themselves?

There was a creak of tortured metal. I turned sharply to Chris who stood still with eyes wide. I looked up to the window and saw the curtains shifting. I pressed hard with my back against the wall. I motioned to Chris and he ducked down behind the car. I watched the pool of light on the ground that shone from the window. I could see Bennett's shadow as he looked out. I held my breath as I watched. I looked towards the fire. It looked like three figures sat there. Margaret had done a good job.

There was a soft beeping sound from within the house. The curtains closed.

I let out the breath I was holding. Our trick had worked. Bennett thought we were all sitting by the fire still.

Then the light in the room was turned off.

Chris was rising from behind the car and I gave him a signal to hold. With my back against the wall, I peered over my left shoulder through the glass sliding door into the entrance hall. I froze as Bennett entered the room. He held a steaming plate. He crossed the room and disappeared behind the bead curtain.

I realised that I had again been holding my breath and I eased it out. I gave Chris the thumbs up to continue his work.

A cool breeze blew across the farm, sending shivers through my body. I looked up at the night sky. Clouds were coming over. We were getting a cool change. Possibly rain. I shivered again and I looked back through the door. The gun again drew my attention. Below the gun was the key rack, and on the key rack hung the keys to Bennett's car. I could have slapped myself. How could I have forgotten Bennett hung the keys in plain view? Gun and keys. Keys and gun. Both of them, right there and within my grasp.

I looked back towards Chris. A frown of consternation covered his features. He was struggling. I looked back into the house. Keys. Gun. If we had them, the whole complexion of this escape changed. I know I promised Margaret not to do anything stupid, but attaining those items was a game changer. There was no time to discuss a plan B, but if the opportunity presented itself, it had to be taken. I decided I had to get them.

I stepped out from the cover of the wall. If Bennett came back through the bead curtain now, I would be in full view. But I needed to take the risk. Attaining the keys and the gun was everything.

I stepped to the sliding door and pressed against it gently. The door gave. It was unlocked. I eased it slowly open, careful not to make a sound, and stepped into the room. I could hear the muffled sounds of the television set from Bennett's room. There was another creaking of metal from outside. I grimaced. Chris was being too loud. I turned and eased the sliding door behind me to limit the sound I was letting in. I stepped towards the counter. I just needed to reach over and take what I needed. The keys and rifle were almost in my grasp.

Suddenly, there was a loud crack. I froze. The television in the bedroom was muted. Everything was still for a moment, and the only thing I could hear was the pulsing of my heart which boomed like a massive bass drum. Then I heard the crunch of a beer can being crushed and a curse. Bennett was coming down the hall!

I looked about me. If I opened the door now, he would hear it. I had no reason to be in here. I panicked and ducked behind the counter. It was stupid. Really stupid. All he had to do was step past the counter and I would be in clear view.

I heard the sound of the bead curtain being pushed aside. I bit my lip. There was only a shoddy wooden counter between Bennett and I. Mere feet between us. I could hear him breathing loudly through his mouth. I waited. Nothing happened. It seemed like an eternity. In and out he breathed. It was torture. Why was he just standing there? I wanted to scream. I clenched my fists and bit my lip harder. Then Bennett snatched something, and was gone.

The bead curtain clicked gently in his wake. The sound of the television set returned. I waited a moment longer, catching hold of my breath and calming my nerves. That had been close. Too close.

I peered around the counter at the curtains. They still waved gently, and I could see cracks of light from the room at the far end of the hall. I eased myself up and peered above the counter. The gun was gone, but the keys remained.

I was just about to reach out to them when I became aware of a soft tapping on the glass. I turned my head to see Chris. He was beckoning me out with urgency. He had the control in his hand. I turned back to the keys, considered them a moment before abandoning my quest.

I eased open the door and closed it again behind me. I admonished myself. I had taken a huge risk, gone off script, I had failed to get the gun or keys and almost been caught. It was a stupid, stupid thing to do.

"What the hell, Paul?" Chris hissed through clenched teeth. "What crazy arsed shit were you trying to pull? You were supposed to keep watch."

I grimaced. I did not need him telling me how bad my decision had been. I was already well aware. "I saw the keys and gun hanging there. I thought it would be easier if I got them, so I went inside. I thought I might try and steal the gun, but I couldn't."

I decided not to say more. I did not want to reveal how I almost blew the entire plan.

"Jesus, Paul" Chris whispered. "You've got balls of steel but the common sense of a lemming."

The temperature had dropped significantly and I shivered as the cold air blow against my damp, sweaty skin.

"So that thing you have in your hand. That is the gate opener?"

Chris smiled. It was the broadest, warmest smile I had seen from him in over a day.

"Sure is. I cracked the window with the wedge, but I got it open." He held the controller up and stuck his tongue out at me. He tucked the control back into his pocket. "Where's Bennett?"

I nodded towards the house. "In his bedroom watching TV."

"Great," said Chris, suddenly seeming as happy as a child on Christmas morning. "Let's go."

He started jogging towards the fire. I paused a moment, still recovering from my scare in the entrance hall. My legs were still shaky and I was not sure I could make it under my own steam. I pushed away from the wall, staggering after Chris.

Chris stopped and turned. The delight of the successful heist was still evident on his face. I gave him a weak thumbs up. I was weary. I really needed to sit down and relax.

Then suddenly I felt it. That strange sixth sense that tickles the back of your mind and tells you something is wrong. Very wrong. I turned back to the house, half expecting to see Bennett framed in the doorway with the gun on his shoulder, looking at us down the sights. But nothing. No Bennett, no gun.

But the awful feeling was still there. I turned back to Chris. He looked at me, confused. Then I saw it. The dark shadow that loomed over him, more than double his height. I saw the two long antennae, which twitched, reaching high into the sky like steel cables on a bridge. The two giant claws, with pinchers as long as Chris was tall, hovering, ready to strike. The shiny black eyes at the front of the head, considering us with predatory hunger. The eight, arachnid legs holding the giant body up. The mouth pieces that moved and clacked and twitched hungrily. And finally, I saw the long, raised tail that ended in a fan.

My jaw dropped and Chris seemed to sense the danger now too. He turned slowly, taking in the giant that stood over him in a menacing fashion.

And then the giant yabby struck.

15

The first claw came down hard on Chris' shoulder to clasp him around his chest. There was a crunch as the yabby tightened its grip, and I saw Chris' chest cave inwardly. The second claw grabbed Chris around the waist. The yabby lifted Chris off the ground and over its head. Chris tried to scream, but only blood came from his mouth. The yabby's claws twitched, twisting Chris' body until his hips sat at right angles to his shoulders. There was a loud, wet snap, and the life went out from Chris' eyes.

The yabby lowered Chris' lifeless body again, bringing its front two legs into range. Each of the front two legs had smaller, claw-like pincers at their ends. These pincers reached out to the body and started cutting through Chris' flesh like scissors cutting through cloth. The yabby cut away the flesh of Chris' stomach and a pile of intestines tumbled out, spilling gore onto the ground. The small front legs flashed about, cutting, grabbing and lifting the innards of Chris' dead body into the hideous, bloody maw of the great beast.

I was stuck with fear, staring as the giant yabby shredded the once affable man named Chris into morsels of meat, which it gobbled down with delight. The horrible splashing, gnawing and clicking on the monstrous yabby's mouth sounded in my ears. I felt sick. I wanted to run. But my legs would not respond. I was stuck fast.

My mind tumbled over as I tried to comprehend the horror in front of me. I remembered the bloodied and torn kangaroo Maisy had found on day one. The strange way she acted around the dam. The empty fields of the farm. There was nothing, literally nothing, around this farm. No domestic animals, and those that were wild had learned to stay away. That first night I heard the gunshot and saw what must have been Bennett, dragging the corpse of the kangaroo for the yabby to feed on.

I thought of the fields, once filled with sheep. I imagined the grisly horror of those poor sheep being picked off, one by one, to sate this monster's hunger. Had that been what had sent this farm down the drain? The feeding of this unfathomable monster?

And then finally I remembered the lockdown, the fences and the gate. The rules. The aggressive behaviour when we were looking for a way out. It was as I had feared. Bennett had made his farm a prison. He invited us in and locked us down. With horror I realised the monstrous truth of it all. Bennett had long since run out of sheep to feed this monster with, so he found a new food supply. A new source of meat. Bennett had not locked us in here to protect us from the pandemic. He had locked us here to feed this yabby.

The clues were all there. My mind had just failed to register it. How could I? A giant, man-eating yabby was far beyond anything I could imagine. It made sense, too, why he was just down at the dam. He must have called it. Supper time!

I turned slowly to look at the farmhouse once more. How could he? How could he invite people in just to be prey for this monster? Was it any surprise, then, that he was so hostile and unfriendly? That he drank so heavily and did not look after his personal hygiene?

But what was their relationship? Was this…thing… his pet?

My mind was working overtime. I turned back to the beast. I needed to get out of here. Get Margaret out of here and to safety. She needed to be a grandmother, not yabby food. I needed to move. Now.

Loose skin flapped like wet curtains and blood poured from the corpse of Chris as the beast continued to feed. I looked into the black, animal eyes of the yabby. Was it watching me? I could not tell.

I took a quick step to the side. The yabby shifted, its six legs pumping the ground as it turned to keep me front on to it.

I took a few quick, shallow, ragged breaths. I could not stay here. I risked a second step, only this time I took it slowly. This time the yabby did not adjust position. I took a few more ragged breaths and stepped slowly once more. Again, the yabby did not move.

I stared up at the beast. It was attracted to fast movement. Perhaps if I moved slowly enough it would let me pass. I looked at the distance between myself and the fire. It was a painstakingly long way.

I took another step.

I was sweating profusely despite the cool air that swirled around me. The air began to smell of rain. It was odd how vivid these details registered so clearly in my mind.

I stepped to the side once more.

My heart was hammering like a jackhammer. I had kept myself fairly fit through regular exercise and daily walks. I had always kept away from sugary snacks and never liked food that was overly sweet. It helped me keep a healthy heart, and I was fortunate as I was now fifty-seven years of age without yet experiencing heart problems. I lifted my hand and placed it against my chest to feel the wild beating of my heart. I never had a problem. Please, God, do not let the first time be now.

Another step.

The beast continued to feed. It had not straightened to face me since the first step. I wondered if it was watching me. I was worried I would take five more steps like this only for it to turn, rendering all my slow progress to date void.

I stepped to the side again.

Would it be better just to run? Or would the yabby's hunter instinct be drawn to the chase, regardless of how hungry it was?

Another step.

What if I waited it out? Just stood here, like an idiot, waiting for it to finish its meal? Would it skulk back to the dam, its appetite sated, or would it come after me as seconds? I could not take the risk. I needed to get to Margaret and then to the motorhome.

Another step.

I was at a right angle to it now. The creature was a marvel, and were I not so taken with fear, I would have looked upon the monster with awe. It was a giant of a thing, a full twelve-foot-high and at least thirty-two feet long from tail to nose. Its muddy brown shell shone wetly in the night.

I stepped to the side again.

My mind was still a mess but a small glimmer of hope started to penetrate my mind. Eight steps now and the yabby had not moved. It had to be something.

The beast continued to click noisily as it fed. Chris' stomach was all but gone now. It had been completely eaten away. I saw one of the front pincers reach up inside Chris' chest to pull out another cut of red mess before placing it in its clicking mouth.

A cloud drifted across the moon and it became suddenly much darker. I took advantage of the temporary cover and took another step.

The sliding door of the house opened. Both the yabby and I turned to the source of the sound. Bennett stood, framed by the open doorway. He was empty handed. The cool breeze hit him, and he pulled his arms around him as he shivered. He paused in the doorway, and I wondered if he could see me when the cloud passed and the moonlight flooded the area again.

"Shit," he swore loudly, and dashed back into the house and through the bead curtain. My immediate thought was that he was running for the gun to get me. I doubted he was getting it for the yabby.

The movement, however, did cause the yabby to turn towards the house and away from me. Facing the yabby's back, I took a punt. I turned and ran.

I used to be a lot faster. Age had gotten the best of me, and nowadays when I ran, it felt like I was trying to run through water. It felt like an eternity, but I quickly reached the fire. There were only pillows on the seats. No Margaret. I heard a car horn. I turned to see Margaret was already in the front passenger seat of the motorhome. I looked back towards the house. The yabby had not moved, but Bennett had reappeared with his rifle.

I ran to the motorhome. My breaths were already coming out raggedly, and my running style was not graceful, marked as it was by regular stumbles and my legs faltered. My ribs ached from the bruising they took yesterday as I sucked in heavy breaths. A gun shot rang out in the night and a fountain of dirt kicked up not far from me. I heard Bennett curse and the clicking of the gun as he chambered another shot.

My legs were pumping and for a long time it seemed I was running but not getting any closer to the motorhome, when suddenly I was there. Margaret had started the vehicle and slid across to the passenger seat. I struggled with the door handle, unable to get my shaking hands to work properly. The door clicked and a gunshot boomed across the campground once more. Something vicious stung my thigh and I felt warm blood start running down my leg.

For a moment I thought my knees would buckle, but I steadied myself. I opened the door and hauled myself into the cab. Pain rippled through my wounded leg, but I gritted my teeth and did my best to ignore it. Seated now, I glanced quickly at Margaret, glad that she had been quick thinking and had the motorhome ready to go.

I shifted the vehicle into gear and pushed down on the accelerator. It was a big, heavy vehicle, not designed for quick acceleration, but it lurched forward and thankfully did not stall. Bennett fired again and a spiderweb of cracked glass appeared on the windshield.

"Get down," I screamed to Margaret.

I turned on the headlights and set them to high beam. I straightened the vehicle to point directly at Bennett, hoping to blind him. He held up his arm to block the blinding light. I noticed, too, the yabby shied away from the light, dropping Chris' corpse to scuttle into the shadows of the night.

I turned the motorhome into the driveway and pressed my foot to the floor. The motorhome shuddered over the rough gravel driveway as it picked up speed.

"Where's the gate opener?" Margaret yelled above the noise.

"In Chris' pocket. We can't go back for it now."

"What are we going to do?"

"Plan B. We're ramming the gate."

I looked into the rear-view mirror. I saw Bennett aiming another shot in the shaky reflection. I turned back to concentrate on steering the motorhome.

The shot rang out.

The motorhome suddenly became very hard to control. He must have hit a tyre. I tried turning the wheel in line with the curve of the driveway but the vehicle was slow to respond. I over-compensated in the turn and the rear started fishtailing. I spun the wheel the other way but it was one over-correction too many and I was long past having control. Margaret gasped and I looked to see the motorhome was veering towards a tree. I tried once last spin of the wheel to try and turn away from it.

There was a loud bang. Whether it was another gunshot or something else, I could not tell. Suddenly the horizon tilted dramatically. The inertia forces on the heavy motorhome had become too much and it was tipping over. There was a heavy crunch and the motorhome landed on its side. My head hit the ground through the window beside me and everything went black.

16

Consciousness came back to me slowly.

The first thing I became aware of was the pain. The sharp stinging of my thigh, the aching of my ribs and the pounding throb of my head. I opened my eyes, and for a few moments my brain failed to comprehend my surroundings. The ground was at right angles to the car. I laid against the door, my head resting against the driver's side window and beyond that, the ground.

I blinked, taking the scene in as my foggy mind tried to recall the sequence of events that led up to this moment. Suddenly, it all came back with stark, terrifying clarity.

I pushed myself awkwardly away from the ground and turned my head. Margaret should have been hanging by her seatbelt in the passenger seat above me. The seat was empty.

I called her name. My throat was dry and I was weak. It barely came out as more than a whimper. I cleared my throat and tried again, this time with more force.

"Margaret," I called. I waited. There was no answer. I tried again.

"Margaret. Where are you, Hot Lips?"

Silence was the only answer I received.

I lay a few minutes, despairing. Chris, Sada and Matsui were all dead. Margaret was missing and I was all alone in a wrecked motorhome. Somewhere outside, Bennett stalked with a gun and a ravenous giant yabby hunted for fresh meat. I wished so desperately for this to be a bad dream. I wanted to wake up and shake this nightmare off. But I could not. This was reality.

I checked my watch. I had not been unconscious long. Long enough for Margaret to disappear, but not too long. If she had left, or been taken away, she would not be far. I had to get up and search for her, before it was too late.

I unclipped the seat belt. I needed to move. I needed to get out of here and find Margaret.

I twisted my body and cried out in pain. I checked my thigh. Thankfully, the bullet had only grazed my leg. It was painful but not critical. I would still be able to walk.

I continued to twist and contort, trying to right myself. I gritted my teeth through the pain and finally, after using the seats as leverage, I pulled my legs from under the steering wheel and righted myself. After further strains and struggles, I eventually stood up.

I felt dizzy and placed my hand against where my head hurt. It felt wet, and when I pulled my hand away, it was crimson with blood. I decided against wiping it, hoping the blood would clot.

I looked through to the back of the motorhome. It looked as though a tornado had blown through it. All of the shelves, the refrigerator and the closets had all opened upon impact, spilling their contents. Amid the messy pile was broken plates and glasses, packages of food, clothing, cutlery, board games and pieces and books.

I climbed through the partition and into the back amid the mess. I tried sorting through the jumble, desperate for an aspirin, but it was useless. I found an unbroken bottle of wine instead. Thankfully it was a screw cap top. I doubted I could find the bottle opener just now. I opened the bottle and took a few long gulps straight from the bottle. I checked the label and took a mental note of it. This one was a keeper.

I found Maisy's whistle as well. For a moment, I stared sadly at it. Maisy was gone. I accepted that now. She had probably become yabby food. It was the most likely outcome. Just like Chris, Sada and Matsui. I considered for a moment keeping the whistle as a memento, but then I put it aside. I did not want to remember how my beloved pet had been killed. I wanted to leave here and forget everything.

On top of the pile I found a broken picture frame. The glass was cracked and I pulled the broken pieces away to get a better look at the picture. It was a photo of Margaret with Jane. It was from the last time Jane had come to visit us. The time they came to announce the pregnancy. They stood outside the motel Jane and

Zheng had stayed in after storming out of our home that fateful night. Zheng must have taken this photo. I had not been allowed to visit them there.

I ran my finger along the lines of Margaret's face. Both Margaret and Jane were smiling in the photo, but I could see the deep hurt and sadness in their eyes. Hurt caused by me and a stupid comment about a mixed-race baby.

Jane may forgive me one day for saying what I said. Maybe not. But one thing I knew. She loved her mother more than anyone else in the world. It pained her to leave Melbourne, and even after a year, they were still talking on the phone every night. They always were, and always would be, best friends forever, no matter the distance they lived apart.

Yes, Jane may forgive me for saying what I said. But she would never forgive me if I abandoned her mother right now. Not that I needed that to drive me. I could not let her die at Bennett's evil hands and become yabby food. No, I could not let that happen. I could not live with that being my beloved wife's fate. I needed to find Margaret.

I pulled the photo from the frame and tucked it into my pocket.

I started sorting through the jumble of mess once more. I needed a weapon if I was going back to the farm to search for Margaret. We did not have anything that seemed suitable. We did not pack for this trip with the view of ever needing to be armed. I cursed myself quietly for not bringing my golf clubs. They may have finally come in handy. In the end, I settled on a large knife. It was the best we had.

I took another drink from the bottle and looked above me. The door was now on the 'ceiling' of the motorhome. I stepped up onto the oven and reached up to the door handle. I had to stretch, but I was able to open the door latch. I jumped, shoving hard at the door. It swung outwards and up. It slowed as it approached ninety degrees, and for a moment I thought I had not hit it hard enough when it passed its peak. The door slammed down against the side of the motorhome, creating a large resounding bang. I paused, listening to the night, worried I may have attracted undue attention. All was silent.

I threw the knife up through the open door. I considered the wine a moment before re-capping the bottle and throwing it too. Finally, I reached up, grabbing the doorway and beginning the painstaking task of hauling myself out.

I paused a moment, sitting on top the motorhome. Physically, I was not up to this. I had only pulled myself out of the motorhome and already my breathing was ragged and coarse. My body ached and moaned, and my head swam a little. I was armed only with a kitchen knife and they had a gun and claws. The odds were stacked against me. But they had Margaret. I was not leaving without her.

I dropped to the ground with a grunt. I retrieved my weapon and bottle. I looked towards the house, but there was no sign of either the yabby nor Bennett. The ground between where I crashed and the farm was quite open. I crouched and jogged towards the house in a similar fashion to how Chris had earlier. I kept my wits about me, glancing about as I jogged. There was no sign of life anywhere.

I got to the house without incident and hid amongst the water tanks. I took a moment to catch my breath as I wondered where to go next. I took another swig from the wine bottle and put it down. That was enough for now.

I peered cautiously out from behind my cover. The sky was quite cloudy, but for the moment the moon was out, and it shone brightly over the campground. Neither of my two quarries could be seen. The torn remains of Chris remained where the yabby had left them. I spied movement down by the dam, but I could not make out what it was.

A cloud passed across the moon and I crept out from the cover of the water tank.

The light from the bedroom in the house was still on. I crawled under the window and paused to listen. I could not hear a sound from within, but I could not discount Bennett from being there. I had to be careful.

I crawled forward and slowly approached the sliding door of the house entrance. I stood, pressing my back against the wall and slowly moved my head past the breach to peer inside. The room was dark and empty.

I moved past the glass panelled door to press against the wall on the opposite side. I peered into the room again. Bennett's keys still hung from the holder.

I stared at them. I had not formulated a plan on how to escape once I had Margaret back. I had not gotten that far. Actually, I had no plan at all. But there it was. The keys to Bennett's car. That was it. A plan. I could escape in Bennett's car.

Then I turned back to the mess that was once Chris. I could only use Bennett's car if I had the remote though, and the remote was in Chris' pocket.

I swallowed. Chris was a torn and bloodied mess. I could barely approach the dead kangaroo without feeling ill. How could I approach the grisly wreckage of someone I had shared laughs and drinks with? Someone who I considered a friend?

But I had to.

It was still dark and I could not see anything about me. I stepped forward, mentally forcing each movement of my legs as I neared the gory debris. I closed my eyes, trying not to focus on the raw meat and exposed bones in front of me. I started thinking of Chris, and how he always came up with new and clever ways of referencing just how big of a dickhead Bennett really was. I tried coming up with some new ones to distract myself.

"He's the grand final winner of the dickhead trophy," I whispered. It was weak, but it was a start.

I stepped forward to stand over the torn-up corpse. His middle section had been completely eaten away and the stark white bone of his spine could be seen. The spine was twisted, and many of the bones had jagged edges. The yabby had come close to tearing him in half.

"He wears the yellow jersey on the Tour de Dickhead," I said softly.

The skin on his chest had been torn away, exposing an empty cavity underneath. All of his inner organs, his liver, his heart, his lungs, literally everything had been removed and eaten. His neck, too, had been torn open, and his head was bent at an unnatural angle. His face, oddly, was untouched. I looked into the cold, dead eyes.

"He was top of the class at dickhead school."

The fleshy parts of Chris' legs had also been eaten away. Gone were his calves and his thighs. Chunks of raw flesh still remained on the bone, glistening in the dim light. His shorts where intact, but completely soaked with blood. With the knife in one hand, I forced his pocket open. With the other hand, I reached inside. It was warm, sticky and wet.

"He graduated with top honours at Dickhead University."

It was the wrong pocket. I withdrew my wet hand and studied the corpse. I would need to turn Chris over. I stabbed the knife into the ground and put my hands on his hips. I gently rolled his body away from me. Only the bottom half moved.

"If you climbed Dickhead Mountain, you'd only find Bennet's flag at the pinnacle."

His lower body turned; I reached into Chris' pocket once more. My fingers closed around the round shape of the remote control, and I pulled it out. I wiped it clean of blood against my shirt and dropped it into my own pocket. I once more looked around. Nobody was in sight. I pulled my knife up and ran to the carport. I ran behind the car to hide. I barely made it when I started throwing up all the wine I had drunk. It spewed forth unabated, coming out both my mouth and nose. Finally, it stopped and I sat for a moment to recover.

It was then, as I got my breathing under control once more, that I heard someone walking on gravel.

17

I was open and exposed in the carport. It was a simple structure. A mere four thin legs holding up a roof to protect Bennett's car from the elements.

The footsteps were close, and there was nowhere to hide. Quickly, I crawled under the car. I saw Bennett's feet approaching from the direction of the dam. He was wearing brown farm boots that were caked with dried brown mud. He walked up to the carport and stopped. He turned, facing away from me.

"Fuck," he muttered, "what a mess."

He put the gun down and leant it against the front of the car. I could see the hilt in front of me. He walked to the shed, just two meters away, and went inside. I stared at the gun a moment longer. It was again beckoning me.

I could hear Bennett banging about and cursing from inside the shed.

I started inching forward under the car. There was just enough clearance for me. I reached my hands forward, one still clutching the knife, and pulled myself forward like a lizard with my legs pushing against the ground behind me. The first push was noisy from the stones shifting under my body, but Bennett continued to clatter around in the shed. The second, I took much more slowly.

I was under the engine now. I reached out. The gun was still out of range. Bennett had stopped banging about. He would not be long now.

I pushed myself forward again, sliding gently against the gravel. My pants caught on something, and I had to reach back and unhook myself. I turned back to the gun and reached out. I touched it with my fingertips. It was a small joy, finally touching the gun at last. As I touched it, it shifted under the gravel. I gasped. I was lucky. It almost fell.

I pushed forward once more. I was close enough to reach out and grab it when Bennett reappeared from the shed. I pulled my hand back quickly. Bennett was whistling and pushing a wheelbarrow in front of him. He picked up the gun, slinging it over his shoulder, and wheeled the barrow over to Chris' body.

Bennett had a shovel sitting in the wheelbarrow, and as he stopped the wheelbarrow, he lifted this out. Ho looked over the body for a moment, before raising the shovel and bringing the blade down hard on the spine. He broke Chris' body in two. He lifted the top of Chris easily and dumped it in the barrow. Chris was no doubt light, now that all his innards were removed. Next, he picked up the legs, dumping them on top of the body. Finally, he used the shovel to pick up the last remaining miscellaneous chunks and spread the dirt about to cover the stain.

Bennett threw the shovel on top of Chris.

"Not so tough now, are we big man," Bennett mocked. "What, suddenly have nothing to say to me? What's the matter, yab' got your tongue?"

Bennett laughed vilely at his own joke, before lifting the back of the wheelbarrow and pushing it down towards the dam.

When he was out of sight, I eased myself out from under the car. I crept out and peered down towards the dam. Bennett was walking as casually as he would have done taking out the trash. A fire burned within me. I was not just going to rescue Margaret. I was going to kill Bennett in the process. He was evil and he had to die.

I walked backwards to the house, keeping my eyes levelled on Bennett. I reached the door and slid it aside. With one last look, I stepped inside the house.

I closed the door behind me. I guess it was out of habit. I was only going to be here long enough to get the keys and get out. But then I heard it. A soft, muffled whimper. It sounded like a woman. My heart leapt. I had assumed Bennett had taken Margaret down by the dam. I had never expected to find her here.

I stopped and listened. I heard the whimper again. It was coming from down the hall. I pushed the bead curtain aside and walked down the hall. I could not believe it. Margaret was here? He probably had her tied up, but I had my knife. I had the remote.

And the keys were still hanging there in the entrance. It would be so easy to escape now. If Margaret was here, we could get the keys and car and be gone before Bennett knew it. I would have to let him go, not kill him in revenge for Chris, but Margaret and I would be away, and that was the most important thing.

I accidentally kicked a discarded beer can aside as I approached the door. The whimpering became frantic, like a crying. I quickened my pace, reaching for the door.

"It's ok Margaret, it's just…"

I stopped.

It was not Margaret.

It was Matsui. She was tied to the bed, naked. Her clothes had been used as bindings and were tied tightly around her wrists and ankles to the bedframe. Her hands and feet were coloured purple red. Another cloth had been tied around her mouth, and she was tied in such a way that her legs were forced open.

"Oh, my dear god," I muttered, rushing forward to cut her bonds. Poor Matsui. Her cheeks were stained with tears and her body bruised. I tried not to think about what abuses Bennett put her through as an even deeper hatred of the man burned through me.

I cut one hand free and set about cutting free her foot. She pulled off the gag and started pulling the tie on her other hand.

"Sada is dead," she said. "That bastard Bennett came into our tent at night and cut his throat while we slept. He pulled me out and tied me up. Then he forced me to watch that…thing… eat Sada. Why didn't you tell me they grew so big? He dumped the rest of Sada in the water and then he brought me here and he…"

"Stop there. Just… leave those details out for now."

She looked at me and nodded. I had freed one foot and now began cutting at the bonds of the other. She wiped her cheeks. I could not imagine the level of trauma she had been forced to endure.

"Where are the others?"

"Chris is dead. Margaret and I tried to escape, but we crashed the motorhome. Now I'm looking for her."

"Bennett?"

"He's alive."

She said something in Japanese. Judging by the venom of her pronunciation, I knew it was something bad.

I finished cutting away the cloth from her leg and passed her the knife. I looked about the room for some clothing. The clothes on the floor had been cut or ripped. I opened the wardrobe and found some t-shirts and pants. They passed the smell test so I passed them to her. She passed the knife back and I turned my back as she dressed. It was too late to protect her modesty, but I still wanted to give her that.

The clothes fit her too loosely, but they would do for now.

We crept back down the hall towards the entrance. We stopped at the room of junk, and Matsui leaned in and grabbed a cricket bat. She was not leaving the house unarmed. I wondered if Bennett was still by the dam. We passed through the bead curtain and glanced outside. We could not see anything from here. I reached out and grabbed Bennett's keys from the key holder.

"What's the plan?" Matsui asked. There was no sadness in her voice now. She was tough. Probably tougher than me.

"I still have to find Margaret. I think she might be by the dam. I need to go down and look. Here, take the keys and drive out. I will meet you at the entrance."

I offered the keys to her but she pushed my hand away.

"No, you need Bennett's car for you and Margaret. Our car has a spare hidden under the rim. I'll get my own car and get out."

I looked at her sceptically. A spare key? I was not so sure about that. I suspected she wanted to take a piece of Bennett out before she left. So did I. I did not force the issue. She was an adult. It was her decision.

Just then, a shadow passed by the door. Bennett!

We froze, expecting him to reappear with his gun raised. Seconds passed. Nothing.

I tiptoed to the door and peered out. I could not see him. I pushed the door open and peered out. Bennett was walking up the driveway towards my overturned motorhome. He had walked completely past us.

I motioned for Matsui to join me.

"He'll soon discover I'm gone from the wreck," I whispered. "We need to move fast. Go quickly to the car and wait for the opportunity to get out of here. Be careful, that yabby is out there somewhere still. I'm going to the dam. I'll meet you at the entrance. If we take too long, just go. Get to Port Augusta and tell the police."

She nodded and I set out jogging towards the dam.

I'd barely gone a few steps when I remembered I still had the remote control. I turned to alert Matsui, but she was gone. It was like she had vanished into thin air. There was only open ground between the farmhouse and her car. She had clearly not gone where I had said.

I whispered good luck and turned away. If Matsui planned revenge, then I would not stand in her way. I only hoped she found success in her endeavour.

18

My short jog to the dam was uneventful and soon I was peering out across the open water. The surface was smooth, and the water dark and impenetrable. I found the dumped remains of Chris by the water's edge. Smaller (normal sized) yabbies had sensed the meat and had begun climbing out of the water and over the corpse. I watched as one scuttled over Chris' face and reached out with one claw to pull at Chris' eyelid. The flesh tore off and I turned away in disgust.

I then noticed one small yabby trying to climb my shoe. I nudged it away. It raised its claws at me aggressively, so I crushed it under my foot. Then I crushed another. There. We were even. Two deaths on either side. I had levelled the ledger.

At least that is what I hoped.

I continued to search the bank, when over on the right-hand side of the dam, I spotted a dark bundle. I watched it for a moment but it did not move. I decided to investigate.

I walked around the edge of the dam. Not too close. The big one could be anywhere. The dark water was so impenetrable it could be scant feet away from me and I would not even know it.

As I rounded the edge, I could see the bundle had a human shape, like a body lying flat on its back with its arms outstretched.

Margaret! Could it be? My heart leapt and I broke into a run. The ground was uneven and I almost tripped. After a few ragged steps, I regained myself and ran on.

I reached the shape and collapsed to my knees in front of it. It was Margaret.

Her hair lay matted across her face and I brushed it aside gently. Her eyes were closed and she looked pale. There was bruising around her left eye, and she had a couple of small cuts and abrasions. I stared a moment, too scared to check her pulse as I feared for the worst. Finally, I reached out and placed two fingers against her neck.

I heaved a great sigh of relief. She had a pulse.

I gave her a gentle shake. I tried rubbing her hand. Talking to her. She was not waking.

I looked back to the farmhouse. There was no sign of Bennett. Yet.

I considered carrying her, but I was far too weak right now. Weariness tugged at my bones and I still had great, throbbing pain coming from my head, ribs and my calf. I considered a moment retrieving the wheelbarrow Bennett had used, but I discarded the thought immediately. Not only would it be slick with Chris' blood, it would also take too much time to retrieve.

A popping noise sounded to my left and I turned to the dam. Some bubbles had appeared on the surface close to the middle. Big bubbles. My sixth sense tingled and I shivered.

I shook Margaret more vigorously this time to wake her. Nothing. I called her name, begging her to wake up. Nothing.

I looked back over the water of the dam. More bubbles appeared. This time they were closer. They were moving towards where I sat.

I dropped the knife, stepped over to the dam and knelt down. I cupped my hands in the water and withdrew them. I walked back to Margaret with the dirty water.

"I'm sorry for this," I said quietly, then dumped the muddy liquid on her face.

She sat up as though electrocuted, coughing and spluttering. I knelt beside her and she hugged me. I wanted to stay in the hug, but a giant predator was approaching. I pushed her away.

"Come on, we need to get out of here."

I looked back at the dam to see two long cables snaking their way across the surface of the water towards us. The yabby's antennae. The beast was coming.

I retrieved the knife and helped Margaret to her feet. She had trouble standing. She had banged her bad knee in the accident and could not put any weight on it. I asked her to hold the knife while I wrapped her arm over my shoulder. I placed my arm around her waist to steady her. She would need to hop alongside as I ran.

The beast's head had broken the surface now and it regarded us with its two big beady eyes. For a moment it was still, then it lurched forward.

"Run," I yelled, pushing forward. Margaret hopped alongside me, trying to keep up with my pace. Behind us, the giant yabby rose from the dam, mud falling from its shell in great sloughs, splashing loudly in the water about it.

We staggered and ran. Margaret hopping and me trying to hold her up and run at the same time. It was ungainly and we were making slow progress, but it was the best we could do.

I dared a glance over my shoulder. The yabby was out of the water now and began scuttling after us on its long, thin legs.

"Faster," I urged, "we need to move faster."

But Margaret was hopping as fast as she could, and I was already at top speed. In fact, I feared I could barely keep up this rate as it was. The bullet wound in my thigh screamed and I was sure it was bleeding again. I pushed Margaret and myself on, shouting encouragement and willing us forward.

I could hear the yabby closing on us. The thumping of its feet on the ground and the wet smacking of its mouth pieces as it craved for our flesh.

We were closing on the shed. The door was wide open. I pointed it to Margaret.

"Let's dive in there, it's our only chance," I panted.

She did not even acknowledge me. She was deeply focused on her hops. In keeping pace with me.

We were closing on the shed fast. The yabby was hot on our heels, but we were going to make it. I could see it. I could feel it. We were going to make it.

And then Bennett stepped out from behind the shed with his gun to block our path.

19

Bennett. Shit.

He raised the rifle to his shoulder and pointed it as us.

I did not know what to do. If we kept running, Bennett would shoot. Stop, and we become yabby food.

I stumbled and missed my footing. We almost fell but rallied. We kept moving towards him. He smiled. That shit eating son of a bitch smiled.

And then I smiled. Because I saw what he could not see.

I knew he saw me smile, because a look of slight confusion crossed his features. A sudden crisis of confidence, perhaps, at my mood shift. It did not matter either way. Matsui stepped from the shadow and swung the cricket bat. The flat of the bat crashed in the rear side of Bennett's head, sending his limp body sprawling. Matsui had hit him with a pull shot that would have made Ricky Ponting proud.

There was no time to celebrate, however, as the yabby was almost upon us. Matsui's eyes widened as she saw the voracious predator chasing us.

"In the shed," I called.

She ducked in. The yabby must have reached for me with its claw because I suddenly heard a loud clack behind me. It spurred me on, and I pushed Margaret harder. We reached the shed and dived forward through the open doorway.

Matsui tried to slam the door shut behind us but was knocked brutally aside as the great yabby smashed the door back open with its monstrous claw. Matsui was momentarily stunned, lying and groaning where she fell.

The yabby reached into the shed, and as I rolled over, I saw the massive claw hovering above me. Then it came crashing down. I rolled aside just in time.

The beast withdrew its claw and tried to look inside the shed. I scrambled to my feet. Margaret groaned. She had not moved since diving through the doorway.

The yabby claw breached the doorway again. This time I could see it was aimed at Margaret. I leaped towards her, grabbing her arms and trying to drag her clear of the claw's reach. I failed.

The claw clamped Margaret on the foot. It held her fast, just below the ankle. I readjusted my grip, holding her under the arms. She wrapped her arms around me. I pulled. Margaret screamed like I had never heard before. And never wanted to hear again.

"I'm sorry, Margaret," I cried and pulled again. The yabby held her tight.

Then it pulled.

It was like trying to hold an accelerating car. It had only been a short pull, but we were dragged like lightweights right up to the doorway. I twisted my body to look up into its cold, beady eyes. Its mouth pieces moved, wet and dripping. I could feel the malevolence of the monster. Its primal hunger. It had already eaten Chris tonight. How greedy could this beast be?

I twisted my body around, still holding Margaret tight. I braced my legs on either side against the door frame.

"What are you doing, Paul?"

"Bracing myself."

The yabby remained still and silent.

"Paul," she said, her voice soft now, "I think you should let me go. Jane needs at least one parent."

Tears welled in my eyes. It could not be me. If Jane was to have only one parent survive, it needed to be Margaret. Not me. I was going to save Margaret or die trying.

"No, Margaret. I'm getting you out of this."

She sobbed. I did not believe me either.

I locked my feet against the door frame. It was probably very stupid of me. The monster was so strong it would break both my legs and pull them from their sockets if it pulled hard enough. But I had no choice. I was not letting go of Margaret.

Then the yabby pulled.

I pulled too. It was strange. There was a millisecond of extreme pressure. Then nothing.

I lay still, my feet against the door frames and Margaret in my arms. I had no idea what had happened. Then Margaret screamed.

I staggered to my feet, pulling Margaret away from the door. Matsui was suddenly at my side helping me. We pulled Margaret a safe distance and then I moved around to inspect her.

It was not as bad as I had feared. The yabby had torn away Margaret's shoe, plus great divots of soft flesh had been ripped from her foot. I pulled my t-shirt off quickly, wiping the blood away to inspect the wound. There were two distinct tears in the flesh, one either side, but there appeared to be no bone damage. It was raw, bloody and painful, and in the back of my mind I could not help but think Margaret may struggle to walk for a long time. But that was not the important thing here. The important thing was that Margaret was still with us.

Matsui must have had some sort of medical training, or at least a better sense of what to do than me. She took the t-shirt away and retied it around Margaret's foot. It still wept blood, but it was tight and it protected the wound.

"I need water," Margaret gasped through clenched teeth. I looked around desperately. There were no taps or hoses in the shearing shed that I could remember. Then I spotted them. Sada and Matsui's drink bottles. I could have slapped myself. Here is where I left them.

Matsui gave me a strange look as I grabbed them, so I held up Sada's bottle.

"Is it ok if we use this?" I asked.

She looked sadly at the bottle a moment before nodding. Margaret gulped the liquid down.

I was slowly catching my breath and started to wonder what the yabby was doing. It had been a few moments of silence. I could see the monster outside. I was standing like a statue. Margaret's stolen shoe lay discarded on the ground.

"Why don't you eat Bennett, you big bastard?" I yelled at it. "Take him and leave us alone."

Its great beady eyes moved. It looked up at the roof. It looked along the wall of the shed. Then it crept on me what the monster was doing. It was looking for weaknesses. It was working out how to break in.

"We need to get out of here," I said.

"No, we are safe for now," Margaret said through gritted teeth. "It can't fit through the doorway. It can't reach us now. We just need to wait it out. At worst, it waits until sunrise before retreating into the dam."

The yabby had other ideas. It stepped back and away, out of the view we had of it through the doorway. I could not say what was worse: seeing it out there, or not knowing where it was. It was up to something. I could feel it. I needed to know.

I started walking towards the doorway.

"Paul, don't," Margaret pleaded, "stay away from there. It could be just behind the corner."

I ignored her and kept walking. I could hear it moving outside. It was still close. What was it doing? I was almost at the doorway when it lashed out.

The resounding boom of impact of claw on sheet metal rang loudly in the shed. The whole shed seemed to shake under the impact, and a huge dent appeared at the point of impact. Dust trickled from above, jolted from its years of rest on the beams. I coughed from breathing in the age-old grit.

The yabby hit again. And again. And again.

The banging resonated loudly inside the shed and I put my hands against my ears. Matsui yelled something, but I could not hear it over the din. I ran to Margaret's side to hold her hand.

"I'm not sure the shed will hold out," I yelled. I could not say if she heard or not.

The yabby struck again with the point of its claw. It must have been a weak spot in the sheet metal, perhaps where bullets had riddled it, because in this moment, the great yabby claw punched completely through the sheet metal. The mighty claw opened and closed, clacking loudly before the monster withdrew it.

We could see the monster clearly now through the hole it created. Worse, it could see us.

It reached one claw to the hole and gripped the side. With a show of strength, it pulled. Metal screamed as the yabby tore the metal wall like a child tearing paper. It tore away a great rent, then gripped at another spot and pulled again. The yabby was literally tearing the wall open before our eyes.

I looked about for another exit. There were a couple of small, low chutes that were used to herd the sheep in and out of. It would require navigating an obstacle course of barriers, races and pens, but if we got there we could easily crawl through and escape. It was our only hope.

I shouted to Matsui and Margaret and pointed to one of the chutes. I was not sure they understood my words but I think the meaning was clear. They both nodded grimly.

The yabby was making short work of the shed wall and we would need to move quickly. Four great strips had been torn away now. The hole was almost big enough for the yabby to squeeze its gigantic body through.

As I went to pick Margaret up, I realised the problem was bigger than I had first thought. The yabby had injured the foot on Margaret's good leg. We were going to need to support Margaret from either side and carry her out. I called Matsui over to help. Margaret winced as we lifted her. I felt my own strength again faltering as I tried shifting her weight into a comfortable position. I checked Matsui was good. She gave a quick nod and we carried Margaret to the first barrier.

The barrier was the walls to one of the pens that lined this part of the shearing shed. The barrier was lined with wooden slats. There was no way through or under the barrier. We would have to lift Margaret over the fencing. It was rib high.

There was another loud crash and the yabby broke through the wall. The hole was not yet big enough to fit its full body through, but through sheer brute force, the yabby was pushing its way in. It slipped its front legs through the breach and with one claw reached for us with a great lunging strike. We dropped to the ground to avoid the snapping claw. The claw clattered against the wooden barrier. A huge chip of wood was cut away.

The claw hovered above us, snapping and clacking as the frustrated yabby tried to grab hold of us.

"Go," Margaret yelled, "I'm too much of a burden. Save yourselves. Go."

It was brave of her, but I could not. Would not. I did not think Matsui could either. We lay there, frozen, as the monstrous claw snapped above us.

The yabby pushed against the wall again. Metal groaned loudly against the force of the yabby as it tried to leverage forward those last few inches it needed to finally clutch us in its deadly claw. The claw snapped shut again. It was less than a foot above us now.

Then I heard another noise.

My mind was too hazy to recognise it at first. But it continued, and slowly my cloudy mind began to comprehend the sound. It was a dog barking. Maisy. She had come back for us.

The yabby paused, then it was gone. Its retreat was startlingly rapid. One moment the claw was hovering there, inches above us, the next moment it was gone.

"What happened?" Matsui asked.

"Maisy," I said, shaking my head as tears started blurring my vision. "She snuck up on it. Yabbies have predators too. Its natural defensive instincts must have kicked in when it realised she was behind it."

We lay quietly and listened. The sound of the barking was diminishing. Maisy was drawing the monster away. I pushed myself to my feet. Every part of my body ached in protest. My head swam and I steadied myself against a pillar before staggering to the doorway. There was no sign of Maisy or the yabby. They were both gone.

Maisy had given us our chance to escape at last.

20

We did not know how long we had. Maisy had led the yabby away, but for how long?

I helped Margaret into a sitting position. She drank more water from Sada's bottle. She was pale. She needed medical attention soon. As did I.

"What's the plan? How are we getting out of here?" she asked.

"I have Bennett's car keys and the remote control to the front gate. We just have to get to his car and drive out of here. We can do it, Margaret. We just need to get to the car. Then we leave. All of us."

She nodded and took another drink from the bottle. I could see in her face that she was steeling herself.

"Ok," she said at last, "let's do it."

Matsui and I hooked her under each arm and pulled her to her feet. She assisted, pushing against the ground with both feet. She winced. I could not imagine the pain she felt.

We were all breathing heavily when we had her up. We took a moment and made our way to the door. It was slow progress. I peered cautiously out. The barks were distant and there was still no sign of the yabby.

"Wait," Margaret said, "get the knife. We might need it still."

A knife? Against a yabby? I did not see the sense in it but I retrieved it from where it had fallen. Margaret held it. It seemed to give her some comfort to have a weapon.

We exited the shed. As we passed the motionless body of Bennett, Matsui gave him a swift kick. I did not blame her. I wanted to kick him myself.

We got to the car without incident. I fumbled in my pocket for the key and unlocked the front passenger side door. We lowered

Margaret in and then swung her legs around to seat her. She looked old and frail as she settled into the seat.

Matsui placed her hand on my shoulder. "You'd better let me drive. You're looking a bit pale."

I was about to protest when my head started to swim once more. The blow I received to my head in the crash earlier was taking its toll. Before I could answer, Matsui had taken the keys from my hand and ushered me into the back seat.

Matsui settled into the driver's seat and adjusted the mirrors. "This is it," she said, "we're going to make it. Any last words before we leave?"

I snorted. "No. Good riddance to this place. Now let's go."

She placed the key into the ignition and turned it. I could hear the engine cranking, but there was no response from the car. It would not start. She stopped and slapped the wheel.

"Give it a moment and try again," I suggested.

Seconds ticked like hours. I peered out into the darkness, expecting at any moment for the yabby to return. I bit my lip nervously.

Matsui tried again.

The engine cranked and coughed. I thought for a second it was about to start but it died. Matsui slapped the wheel and let out a burst of Japanese words.

"It's ok," I said, trying to calm her. "Try one more time."

She turned the key once more, but it was no good. The engine would not fire.

"It's no use. I'll have to get my car," she said.

I leaned forward and crouched to see her car parked in the campground ahead of us. It was not far, but I did not fancy going out there.

"I don't think we can carry Margaret all that way," I said.

"No, I'll go alone. I'll bring the car here and we will transfer Margaret across then."

"Are you sure you want to go out there alone?"

Matsui turned and gave me a bleak smile. "It's ok. We don't have a choice. Besides, the yabby is gone. I'll only be a minute."

She did not give space for any sort of protest. In less than a second, she had opened the door and was gone.

I sat back in my chair. I ran my hand through my hair. I felt the dried, crusted blood from my wound. The car had worked fine when Bennett drove it to Port Augusta. I remember hearing it when he parked it in front of the house upon his return. Of course, that was it. He parked it, then later started it and parked it here. You should never run a car for such a short time. The engine. It must have been flooded.

"How are you feeling, Paul?" Margaret asked.

"I've been better. How are you going, Hot Lips?"

"Oh, ok. I could do with a lie down, I suppose."

I leant forward and placed my hand on her shoulder. She placed her hand on mine. It felt good.

I looked through the windscreen to watch Matsui. She covered the ground quickly, reaching the small SUV in a short space of time. It was parked face on to where we now sat. She crouched down by the front wheel, placing her hand inside the bodywork and feeling under the front fender.

She withdrew her hand and held up a key in our direction like she was holding a trophy. It was a smart trick. They would never be locked out of their car.

The blinkers flared yellow as she unlocked the car.

"Did you see that?" Margaret said.

"See what?" I asked, suddenly apprehensive. A chill ran down my spine.

"When the blinkers flashed, I thought I saw something behind the car."

"Saw what?" I asked again, an edge creeping into my voice.

But Margaret did not need to answer.

I looked up as Matsui started the car. The vehicle's lights came on and I saw it too. It was clear in the dull red glow of the rear brake lights.

The yabby had returned.

21

We could see Matsui in the car facing us through the windshield. She was leaning over and looking for something in the glove box. She slammed it shut and started looking in the middle compartment.

The yabby scuttled around to the driver's side of the SUV, sizing up its prey. Its head was scant feet away from Matsui, who searched on through the compartment, blissfully unaware.

"What the hell is she doing?" I asked, my voice suddenly shaky. "Move, Matsui. *Move.*"

Margaret leaned across and tooted the horn. She gave it three loud blasts.

Matsui looked up. She stared at us for a moment, raising her hands as if in question. She had no idea the yabby was there.

The yabby attacked.

The yabby's claw smashed hard against the side of the car. The windows shattered and Matsui was showered with broken glass. The SUV rocked under the impact. Matsui screamed. She put the SUV into gear and it started to roll forward when the yabby clutched the vehicle with its claw. She slammed the accelerator and the front wheels began kicking up dirt as they spun. But the yabby held tight and the vehicle did not move. I could see the top tip of the claw had penetrated the panelling on the door under the yabby's grip.

The yabby lifted the SUV, tipping it over and onto its side. It landed with a crunch. Matsui screamed again as she tumbled down the vehicle into the passenger seat. The yabby mounted the vehicle, its spindly legs holding the car steady so as not to turn it over completely. With a sharp pull, the yabby pulled the driver's side door away.

"My god," Margaret whispered under her breath.

The yabby pushed its claw down through the open doorway, reaching down to grab at Matsui.

"Margaret, don't watch."

Matsui raised her legs, trying to kick the claw away. There was little room for the yabby's giant claw to manoeuvre, and the claw snapped just above Matsui's chest. She squirmed and tried to punch the windscreen out with her bare fist. She battered it, screaming. I watched on helplessly. There was nothing I could do.

Then the yabby had her.

The claw clamped down on an outstretched leg and held fast. In an instant, Matsui was hoisted out of the SUV and dangling in the air before the giant yabby's greedy eyes. The yabby held her there for a moment. Matsui struggled, blood running from where the claw held her tight. The yabby drew her close, bringing her within range of the smaller front legs. The front legs whipped forward, and there was an explosion of blood.

I buried my face in my hands. I had seen enough of this already. The grotesque way the yabby tore its victims apart to feed. I remembered all too vividly how those small claws on the front legs had cut through Chris' flesh. How his innards had fallen out.

"Paul, we need to go. Can you start the car?"

I thought I could.

I pulled my hands away and looked at the yabby. It remained standing atop the SUV, tearing Matsui to shreds. I eased the door open and stepped out of the car. I remembered how quick movements drew the yabby's attention and slow ones did not. I moved as slow as I could. I closed the rear door with a click. The yabby stopped. I froze.

The yabby climbed down from its perched position. The limp body of Matsui hung in its claws, her head lolling from side to side as it dismounted the SUV. It paused a moment on the ground. I sensed it watching me. Considering me.

Then it turned, carrying its prey towards the dam. I heaved a sigh of relief. Perhaps it had eaten enough for the night.

I opened the driver's door and stepped into the car. Matsui had left the keys in the ignition.

I turned to Margaret. She looked very pale and weak. Her foot wound was still leaking blood and there was a growing blood stain on the carpeted floor of the car.

I pushed the accelerator to the floor and turned the key. I let the engine crank for ten seconds, listening for the moment the engine tried to start. It coughed and I switched the ignition to off again.

"You're doing no better," Margaret grumbled.

I turned the key once more. The engine started. I let out a whoop. There was a strong petrol smell to the air and black smoke poured from the tailpipe, but I had started it. I revved the engine a few times loudly. Margaret slapped my arm.

"You're going to draw that thing's attention."

"I need to burn off the excess fuel or it will stall."

I revved a few more times and turned on the headlights. They lit up the grisly scene of Matsui's murder in full. Blood and gore had splashed the car, dripping down the windscreen and sides of the car. A red chunk of something still sat where the yabby perched on top. Thankfully, the yabby was gone.

I pulled out of the carport and eased up the driveway. After the carnage that had passed, the world seemed oddly peaceful in this moment.

Ahead was the site of the crash and our once beautiful motorhome. I eased the car around it, looking at it as we passed and amazed at how we both survived the crash.

"Did you want to stop and salvage anything?" I asked.

"No, let's just go."

I rounded the motorhome and steered back onto the driveway. Ahead of us was the gate. The last obstacle between us and our freedom.

I pulled the remote control from my pocket and passed it to Margaret.

"Would you like to do the honours?"

She took it with a weak smile and pointed the control at the gate. She pressed the button. For a second, nothing happened. My heart began to sink at the thought of having to return back to the house. Then it moved. Slowly, but it was moving.

The gate came to a stop. I was struggling to believe it. The end was in sight. I eased the car forward and we had finally done it. We passed through the gate and were out of Spear Creek Farm. We were free at last.

I eased the car up to the main road and stopped. I killed the ignition.

Margaret sat up in her seat. "What is it, Paul?"

"Maisy. I can't leave her here. Not after she saved us back at the shed."

Margaret nodded slowly, turning it over in her mind.

"And how will you find her?"

"The whistle. It's in the motorhome. I just need to get it and…" I was blabbering.

Margaret stared ahead at the empty road.

"Ok, Paul," she said at last, "go and get Maisy back."

22

It felt like madness stepping back through the gate to Spear Creek Farm, but here I was.

I took a deep breath and passed through the threshold. It was strange how one step either side made the world feel so different.

I walked steadily towards the van. The night was silent. Not even a bird sounded. Everything seemed oddly still. It made me nervous. I wished I still had the knife, but I had left it in the car with Margaret.

I reached the motorhome without issue. I circled the vehicle once, quickly, searching for the best spot to climb it. In the end, I decided to climb the underside. There were more parts to hold and put my foot in for leverage.

I reached the top and collapsed. My body was not used to this level of stress and exertion. Once we got out of this, I would probably sleep for a week.

I pushed myself across the side of the motorhome until I reached the door. I turned and dangled the lower half of my body into the motorhome. I took a couple of deep breaths and lowered myself in.

I landed on the oven and looked about. The inside was unchanged. It was still a mess.

I found the whistle where I had left it and thrust it in my pocket. I sorted through the jumble more and was able to find a couple of undamaged bananas. I tucked these into my other pocket. Then I looked for food for Maisy. She had been lost a few days. She would be starving. I sorted through the mess and found a defrosted steak. That would do.

I climbed back up onto the oven and reached up to grab the doorway. I hauled myself out of the motorhome. It was a lot harder than I remembered from the first time I did it.

I sat on the top a moment to rest. I desperately needed to lie down.

"Almost there," I assured myself.

I blew on the whistle as hard as I could.

I heard nothing, of course. But Maisy should have heard. Maisy was bound to come.

I climbed down the motorhome and walked around to get a better view of the farm. It was so serene in this moment. Everything was quiet and at peace now the carnage of the night was over.

The cool breeze blowed gently and I looked up, wondering when the rain would come. The wind rustled the leaves on the tree by my right, and I closed my eyes a moment to enjoy the peace.

Then I heard the dry snap of a twig breaking.

I turned to the tree to see Bennett emerging from the shadows. His eyes were red lined and bloodshot, but there was no mistaking the murder in them. He carried the gun in his hands.

"Paul," he mocked, "you almost made it. You almost got away."

I turned to face him, raising my hands to show I had no weapon.

He chuckled as he stepped further into view. His gait was unsteady, but he still held a gun.

"You know Paul, of all the visitors I've had here, you've been my toughest. I never had anyone get this far before. I congratulate you. Very well done for an old man."

I was not sure if it was a compliment or an insult. Especially the spiteful way he spat the words 'old man'.

"So, this is it," I said, trying to sound casual but failing miserably, "this is what you do. Invite travellers in and feed it to that...thing?"

He smiled a smile that beamed both confidence and malevolence at once. "Of course, Paul. What else is there to feed it? I ran out of sheep some time back."

"You couldn't just drive down to the butcher's shop?"

He smiled, almost as if he enjoyed the banter. "Not with her appetite."

I was stalling. Delaying. Trying to stay alive longer. Hoping for a miracle.

"So, what's in it for you then, Bennett? That thing, is it your pet or something?"

"What's in it for me?" he repeated, seeming surprised to hear the question. He smiled. "I'll tell you what's in it for me. I get to kill people."

His words chilled me to my core. I had been under some impression that Bennett was somehow doing it all out of need. For a pet. Or out of fear of being eaten himself. All that jumble of a mess in his house. The drinking. I had seen those as signs of mental disturbance. A man living in fear. Or guilt.

But Bennett was not forced. He never was.

Bennett was a serial killer.

The realisation that came over my face amused him. He chuckled. "So now you see, Paul, that you too will die. You've left me quite the fucking mess to clean up. I have no idea how I'll right that van of yours for starters."

He shook his head and raised the gun to his shoulder and looked down the sight to my chest.

Suddenly there was a growl. We both turned to see Maisy running up the driveway towards us. Her teeth were bared, and she opened her mouth wide as she leaped at Bennett, aiming for his throat. The gun boomed.

I lurched forward to tackle him but Bennett knocked me aside with the butt of his rifle. The blow connected me on the jaw and I momentarily saw stars. I collapsed to my knees and he stepped over me. He chambered another bullet.

A few feet away, Maisy lay in a widening pool of blood, panting heavily. Her eyes met mine and she whined softly.

A tear dropped from my eye and I looked up at Bennett with hatred. He smiled victoriously and levelled the gun to my head. I looked down, not wanting my last sight to be his repulsive face. I just hoped Margaret would get away. That was all that mattered now.

"Goodbye, Paul," Bennett said, "I can't say I'll miss you."

23

Seconds passed as I waited for the end. Tears spilled from my eyes as I thought of Margaret, of Jane, of our soon to be born grandchild that I would never live to see.

People say you see your life flash before you at the moment of death. I did not see my life. I only thought of my regrets. Mistakes I had made. Decisions I could not rescind. Words I could not take back.

Who cares if Jane and Zheng's baby would come out looking more Chinese than Caucasian? I certainly did not. So why did I say it? I will never know. I knew the moment Jane stormed out I would live to regret those words to my dying day. And it was true, because here it was. My dying day.

My tears hit the earth as I waited for the final shot. If Bennett was delaying to torture me, then it was working.

Then Bennett grunted and fell to his knees. The rifle clattered to the ground. I looked up to see Bennett falling towards me. I caught his body and pushed it away. It dropped to the ground. A large stain of blood was spreading from the middle of his back.

I looked up. Margaret stood in front of me. She held a bloodstained knife in her hand. She was shaking.

"Margaret," I cried, climbing to my feet. She dropped the knife and hugged me. I squeezed her tightly then pushed her away.

"Margaret, you shouldn't have come. Your foot, your knee… you shouldn't have risked your life like that. All you had to do was drive."

She frowned, then reached forward and pinched my arm. I knew those signals.

"What?" I pleaded. "What have I said wrong this time?"

"Paul, stop being such a chauvinist. You've been risking your life to save me all night. Stop thinking it's only a man's job to save their spouse. Women are allowed to risk their lives to save the ones they love too."

I gave her a soft smile. "It's called chivalry, Margaret. Besides, Jane needs you more than she needs me."

She waved my comment away as though shooing an annoying fly. "She needs her father too." I went to speak but she quickly held up her hand to stop me. "Don't say it, Paul" she continued, "she *will* forgive you. She needs us both. She knows it. She misses you, Paul."

There was a whine and we turned to see Maisy lying in the dirt, wagging her tail weakly. The stain of blood was continuing to spread around her.

"Now, I don't want to hear any more of it. We need to get Maisy into the car now and get going to Port Augusta if we're to save her."

With effort, I climbed to my feet and nodded.

"Alright. You are right. Let's go."

EPILOGUE

I sat in the waiting room of the hospital. Nobody sat within one and a half meters of me. There were marked locations where we were and were not allowed to sit. This was social distancing, a strange new concept that had become the norm since we had gone into lockdown.

Orderlies and nurses passed back and forth. I watched them go about their business. All wore masks, regardless of whether they attended a patient or not. Opposite me, a child sat in his father's knee, playing a game on a mobile phone. The boy and his father both wore a mask. The boy caught me staring. He pulled down his mask to poke his tongue out at me.

I checked my watch. It had been almost an hour since Margaret had left. I was not impatient. I would wait here all day for her if she wanted me to. I just wished she would give me an update.

I began staring at the vending machine. The prices were outrageous. I started doing the math in my head. I guessed they were making at least two dollars per can. How many cans could the machine hold? How much would it make per day? I started turning the math over in my head when I heard my name. It was Margaret.

"Paul, Jane wants you to come in. She wants you to come and meet your baby granddaughter."

My vision blurred and I wiped away the tear that dropped down my cheek.

"Really, Margaret?"

"Yes, really."

I stood up. My legs were unsteady. Margaret took my arm and guided me forward. I was not even this nervous when I was facing the giant yabby.

I entered the room. Jane lay on the bed holding a small bundle. Jane looked positively radiant. Zheng sat on the edge of the bed, leaning forward to her, touching the bundle gently. Jane looked up and beckoned me over.

"Dad," she said in a voice that broke my heart, "come over here. I want you to meet your granddaughter."

I looked back to Margaret for reassurance. She nodded. Yes, this was really happening.

I stepped forward and Jane turned her for me to see her face for the first time. Her face was that of a yabby.

I woke with a start. Sweat poured from my armpits and brow, yet the house was cool. Margaret continued to snore softly at my side. Her crutches were leaning against the wall. I stood up, remembering the dream. It did not require much effort. It had been the same dream every night now. Every night since we left that God forsaken farm.

Maisy slept at the foot of the bed and I stepped carefully over her legs as I passed her by. She was recovering steadily and was almost her old self again. She hated wearing the cone over her head though.

I walked into the kitchen to get a glass of water. Zheng was there. He had my little granddaughter cradled in one arm as he heated milk in the microwave. I gave him a nod of greeting.

"Up again, Paul? The same dream?"

My granddaughter grizzled grumpily in his arms.

"Yes, the same dream again. Do you need a hand?"

"Sure, could you hold her so I can check the milk properly?"

"I'd love to."

Zheng passed her across. She let out a small cry. Her face was curled up, the distress of hunger and not being able to effectively communicate that very fact was evident in her face. I tried cheering her up with silly faces and smiles but she wanted no part of it. She was too hungry.

It was hard to believe it was not so long ago that I thought this day would never come. Jane had my hard-headedness and seemed unlikely to forgive. But the events at Spear Creek Farm had changed everything.

When the news service finally broke the story, they never mentioned the yabby. They only spoke of the serial killer who owned the farm. I often wonder if the authorities even believed us about the yabby. They said they had dredged the dam. They found more bodies, which they linked to missing people, but no yabby. After a time, Margaret and I got sick of the cynical looks we received and stopped telling the story.

But I worried. I worried where the yabby might have gone. We had left in such a hurry that we had left the front gate open. Maybe it had left the farm altogether. Perhaps that's why they never found it.

Zheng tested the milk temperature on his arm and passed me the bottle. I gave him a questioning look and he nodded.

I watched as my granddaughter gulped greedily at her drink. I almost felt like crying again, as I had done the first time I had seen her. I had never seen such a beautiful baby as her.

"Zheng, I just wanted to say how thankful I am for you letting me back into your lives."

Zheng waved me away. "Paul, please. Jane and I want you in our lives. My parents live far away in China. We want her to grow up with a strong sense of family around her. We need you and Margaret in our lives."

We watched her drink in silence, listening to her soft breathing and the small grunts of effort she made as she swallowed.

"So," Zheng said after a moment, "a repetitive nightmare. Do you think it might have a meaning?"

"Hard to say," I responded.

I had not told anyone what the dream was. How could I? What if it was interpreted incorrectly as being about the baby? That some deduced it might mean I found her ugly?

I had been thinking about the dream a lot since it started happening. A lot. And I think I knew what it meant. It related to the other thing that plagued me from that fateful night. I was not sure I had seen it correctly at the time, but as I think back on it now, I am sure I saw it.

It was when the yabby climbed Matsui's car. The light was limited, and it could have been a trick of my imagination. But the more I think of it, the more I am sure I saw it. It was a moment where the yabby turned, and for a short moment the underside of the yabby's tail became visible. And that's when I saw them. Round, shiny and bulbous. I swear now I saw them under her tail. The hundreds of basketball-sized yabby eggs.

The End